"Ma'am—"

She pointed a finger at him. "I don't like your tone when you call me ma'am."

"I clocked you at eighty-five and it's a sixty-five-mile-an-hour zone that drops to forty-five as you come into town." He paused then added, "Ma'am."

Sparks raced across Sienna's skin. Somehow his tone had gone from patronizing to sexy-as-hell in one word. She had no idea what had possessed her to try to goad this small-town sheriff into a reaction, but her body's response to him was totally unexpected.

And bothersome.

"I'm sorry," she repeated. "This isn't my car so I'm not used to how it drives."

"Who does the car belong to?"

"I don't know." She flipped open the glove compartment. "I assume it's a rental. I took it from my ex-boyfriend."

The sheriff leaned forward, his hands resting above the driver's-side window. The fabric of his shirt pulled tight across his arms, revealing the outline of corded muscles. "As in you stole it?"

"No," she answe⬚⬚⬚⬚⬚⬚⬚⬚⬚⬚⬚⬚⬚te like that." She cl⬚⬚⬚⬚⬚⬚⬚⬚⬚⬚⬚⬚ath.

In fact, it was exa⬚⬚⬚⬚⬚⬚⬚

CR⬚
Finding hom⬚ ⬚⬚⬚⬚⬚ ⬚n the West

Dear Reader,

Welcome back to Crimson, Colorado! This charming mountain town is about to get turned on its ear when Sienna Pierce blows in with a Rocky Mountain—sized chip on her shoulder. She's here to prove to her estranged father and brother that she won't be forgotten so easily this time around.

Free-spirited and unpredictable, Sienna does crazy things to Sheriff Cole Bennett's priorities and neither expects the sparks that fly whenever they're together. As she spends time in Crimson and reconnects with her family, Sienna slowly comes to realize having a home and people who will always stand by her side is possible.

And the man she wants closest to her is the town's sexy sheriff. But Cole keeps Sienna at a distance no matter how close she tries to get in. She can't seem to break through the walls around his heart, and Cole will have to learn to trust both Sienna and himself to claim the love he desperately craves.

I hope you have as much fun reading about their journey to a happily-ever-after as much as I did writing it. Let me know at www.michellemajor.com or through Facebook or Twitter.

Big hugs!

Michelle

Coming Home
to Crimson

—

Michelle Major

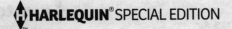

ISBN-13: 978-1-335-46581-8

Coming Home to Crimson

Printed in U.S.A.

www.Harlequin.com

Michelle Major grew up in Ohio but dreamed of living in the mountains. Soon after graduating with a degree in journalism, she pointed her car west and settled in Colorado. Her life and house are filled with one great husband, two beautiful kids, a few furry pets and several well-behaved reptiles. She's grateful to have found her passion writing stories with happy endings. Michelle loves to hear from her readers at michellemajor.com.

Visit the Author Profile page
at Harlequin.com for more titles.

To Jan and Suzanne:
Thank you for being the best aunties a girl
(or her kids) could ever imagine!!

Chapter One

Unfaithful dirtbag. Cheating scum ball. Two-timing lowlife.

Idiot.

A slew of descriptive and mainly colorful phrases pinged through Sienna Pierce's mind. That last word, though, she reserved for herself as she sped along the two-lane highway toward Crimson, Colorado. She'd left the ritzy mountain town of Aspen, and her boyfriend—ex-boyfriend now—in her rearview mirror.

She was an idiot for not seeing the signs earlier. Kevin's late nights at the office, the last-minute business trips, the fact that they hadn't had sex in... Well, she should have guessed something was wrong between them.

But he fit her world—her mother's world. Kevin was her stepfather's heir apparent at the investment firm. She never thought he'd jeopardize his future this way. Although what did it say about their relationship that she'd believed their strongest bond was his career aspirations?

Another wave of humiliation washed over her, bringing with it a mix of sweat and nausea. Interesting that embarrassment and anger were the most prevalent emotions right now. Her stomach churned, but her heart remained relatively untouched.

Did that prove she deserved the ice princess accusations Kevin had hurled at her across the hotel room as he'd rushed to pull up his boxers, while the woman in his bed hid under the Egyptian cotton sheets at the five-star hotel?

She adjusted the temperature inside the Porsche, cold air blasting from the vents in the dash. Perspiration continued to bead all over her body, droplets snaking down her spine. Her long hair clung to her neck, and she pulled it over one shoulder.

The weather on this June morning was perfect, the sky overhead an expansively brilliant blue she rarely saw in downtown Chicago. Mountains rose up to meet the sky to the west, their massive rocky peaks reminding her that she was just a speck on the earth in comparison. Sunlight beat down on the cherry-red sports car, the glimmering reflection mocking both her mood and the fact that at twenty-seven years old, she seemed to be having a premature hot flash.

With one hand on the steering wheel, she tried to shrug out of her tailored Calvin Klein suit jacket, the one that had always made her feel both powerful and sexy, like she could handle anything. Until forty-five minutes ago, when her professional attire and meticulously straightened hair had somehow given the appearance that she was trying too hard compared to the effortlessly seductive woman she'd caught glimpses of in that hotel room.

Nothing in her life was right at the moment, especially when one of her arms got tangled between the jacket's sleeve and the seat belt. The car swerved as she yanked her arm, and she forced a deep breath. Oncoming traffic was pretty much nonexistent between the two towns, which was a bonus since the last thing she needed was to cause an accident.

Pull it together, she told herself as she lifted her foot from the gas pedal. How fast had she been driving anyway?

The answer to that question came as she glanced into the rearview mirror and saw red and blue lights flashing behind her. She let out a little growl, the thought of a speeding ticket fueling her temper.

This was Kevin's fault, too. At least Sienna blamed him. She blamed him for everything.

Dust billowed around the Porsche as she pulled onto the shoulder and parked. She unfastened the seat belt and shrugged out of her jacket. It felt like shedding a thousand-pound wool coat.

Knuckles rapped on the window, and she pressed the lever at the same time she leaned closer to the air vents.

"I'm sorry, officer," she said automatically, fanning her hand in front of her face. "I was having a bit of trouble taking off my jacket around the seat belt. I'll be more careful."

"License and registration, ma'am."

The rumbly voice gave her pause and she sat back, glancing up into the face of a man who could have been the direct descendent of some Wild West lawman. The firm set of his jaw and rugged good looks seemed like a throwback to the era of John Wayne, although he wore a modern law enforcement uniform of a beige button-down and black tie, khaki pants and a gun clearly tucked into the holster at his waist.

The button clipped above his shirt pocket read Sheriff. Okay then, the real deal.

And not feeling all that friendly, if the tight line of his mouth was any indication. She couldn't see his eyes behind the mirrored aviator sunglasses but imagined he was glaring at her.

"Of course," she said and pulled her wallet out of the Louis Vuitton purse on the passenger seat.

"You know texting and driving is against the law," he said as she handed him her driver's license.

"I was having some sort of bizarre hot flash," she blurted. "Not texting." Even now she could feel the silk tank top clinging to her skin. "Anger induced, not hormonal," she felt compelled to add, her cheeks flaming.

One thick brow lifted above the frame of his sunglasses, and Sienna resisted the urge to fidget.

"You were also driving twenty miles above the speed limit."

"I certainly was not." Sienna rolled her eyes. "I'd never drive that fast."

"Ma'am—"

She pointed a finger at him. "I don't like your tone when you call me ma'am."

"I clocked you at eighty-five and it's a sixty-five mile an hour zone that drops to forty-five as you come into town." He paused, then added, "Ma'am."

Sparks raced across Sienna's skin. Somehow his tone had gone from patronizing to sexy-as-hell in one word. She had no idea what had possessed her to try to goad this small-town sheriff into a reaction, but her body's response to him was totally unexpected.

And bothersome.

"I'm sorry," she repeated. "This isn't my car so I'm not used to how it drives." The truth was she'd been too preoccupied with mentally trash-talking her cheating ex-boyfriend to realize she was driving recklessly. Kevin's fault, as well.

"Who does the car belong to?"

"I don't know." She flipped open the glove compartment. "I assume it's a rental. I took it from my ex-boyfriend."

The sheriff leaned forward, his hands resting above the driver's side window. The fabric of his shirt pulled tight across his arms, revealing the outline of corded muscles. "As in you stole it?"

"No," she answered immediately. "I… It wasn't quite like that." She closed her eyes and drew in a breath. In fact, it was exactly like that.

She'd taken a private shuttle from the Aspen airport to the upscale hotel where Kevin had made a reservation. She'd originally been scheduled to come on this trip with him, three days in the mountains of Colorado with a few meetings thrown in to make it a legitimate business expense. Sienna hadn't been back to Colorado in almost two decades, and to make a trip so soon after her estranged brother's visit to Chicago last year… Well, it had been too much to even consider.

Yet in the end, she couldn't stay away. Kevin had acted so disappointed she wasn't coming, dropping subtle hints that he'd planned to pop the question in Aspen. So she'd taken a red-eye into Denver, then a commuter plane to Aspen, thinking how fun it would be to surprise him.

She'd surprised him all right, in bed with another woman. Could it get more clichéd than that? Her life had been reduced to a cliché.

"How about we start with the registration?" the sheriff asked, his voice gentling as if somehow he could sense what a mess she was on the inside.

That infuriated her even more. Sienna didn't do vulnerable. People around her saw what she wanted them to see, and the thought that this mountain-town Mayberry lawman could see beyond her mask made her want to lash out at someone. Anyone. Sheriff Hot Pants, for one.

She dipped her chin and looked up at him through her lashes, flashing a small, knowing smile. "How about I write a healthy-size check to the police foundation or your favorite charity…" She winked. "Or you for that matter and we both go on our merry way?"

"Are you offering me a bribe?"

She widened her smile. "Call it an incentive."

The sheriff took off his sunglasses, shoving them into his front shirt pocket. His eyes were brown, the color of warm honey, but his gaze was frigid. "How's the thought of being arrested as an incentive for you to hand me the registration?"

He smiled as he asked the question. His full lips revealed a set of perfectly straight teeth in a way that made him look like some sort of predator. "Or perhaps you'd like to step out of the car and I'll handcuff you? Another viable option, *ma'am*."

Blowing out a breath, Sienna grabbed the stack of papers from the glove compartment. She hated that her fingers trembled as she leafed through to find the registration card.

She held it up without speaking, and the sheriff plucked it from her fingers.

"Do you have anything else you'd like to say before I run your information?" he asked conversationally.

"I might like to call my lawyer in Crimson," she answered automatically. It would be just her luck that Kevin the scumbag had reported his rental car as missing after she'd convinced the bellman to release it to her. It had felt like a tiny sliver of retribution for what he'd done but now it was coming back to bite her in—

"You have an attorney in Crimson? I find it hard to believe you have ties to anyone in my town."

"*Your* town," she muttered. "Like you own it."

"Ma'am." This iteration was a warning.

"I do know an attorney," she snapped before he could say anything more. "Jase Crenshaw."

The sheriff laughed. "*You* know Jase?"

The way he asked the question made her feel two inches tall. As if Jase Crenshaw wouldn't want anything to do with a woman like Sienna. Which was both ridiculous and possibly true at this point.

But she didn't let him see her doubt. Never show anyone the doubt.

Instead she flashed another smile. "I certainly hope I know Jase. He's my brother."

Cole Bennett blinked. Once. Twice. He rubbed a hand over his jaw, then pulled the sunglasses out of his pocket and returned them to his face.

If the gorgeous and obviously high-strung blonde in the Porsche had told him her brother was the President, he wouldn't have been more surprised.

He patted his open palm on the top of the car. "Sit tight."

"Are you going to call Jase?" she asked, her voice suddenly breathless.

"I'm going to run your plates and make sure this car hasn't been reported stolen."

She snorted, a strangely appealing sound coming from a woman who looked so uptight he guessed she'd never made a noise that wasn't appropriate for a luncheon at a ritzy country club. Living in the mountains of Colorado,

Cole had little use for anything fancy, even with Aspen an easy thirty-minute drive down the road.

"My cheating, dirtbag, sleazeball ex is probably too busy entertaining his mistress to even realize the car is gone."

Cole was amused despite himself. "And when he does?"

She rolled her pale blue eyes. "I *borrowed* the car. I'm planning to return it."

"I gather you recently discovered the cheating, dirtbag, sleazeball side of him."

"Along with a view of his saggy, naked butt in bed with another woman—that part I could have done without."

"How long did you date?"

"A little over two years."

"And his saggy butt came as a surprise?"

She laughed, low and husky, and he felt it all the way to his toes. "I got good at not looking. He had other redeemable qualities."

"Fidelity wasn't one of them?"

He regretted the question when the corners of her mouth turned down. He liked seeing her smile and got the impression she didn't do it half as much as she should.

"Apparently not."

"Do I need to confiscate the keys so you don't take off?" he asked conversationally. "I'm not in the mood for a car chase today."

She met his gaze, her blue eyes sparking with some emotion he couldn't name but that resonated deep in his gut. "Do I look like a flight risk?"

"You look like ten kinds of trouble," he answered, then turned and headed for the Jeep he drove while on duty. Cole Bennett didn't need trouble in his life, no matter how appealing a package it came wrapped in.

Both the car and the woman checked out fine, but Cole didn't trust that things wouldn't go south when the ex-boyfriend realized the car was gone. Maybe she was indeed going to return it, or maybe she was going to do something stupid that would end up bad for all of them.

Cole prided himself on his ability to read people and situations. It was a skill he'd learned first in the army and then through a more recent career in law enforcement. But Sienna Pierce was an enigma.

On the surface, she was a perfect, polished society type—the kind of woman he would have looked right through on any given day. But a current of something more ran just below the surface—a feral energy he didn't quite understand but that drew him despite his better judgment.

He glanced through the front window of the Jeep to the Porsche and sighed. He could call Jase and dump this problem onto his friend's doorstep. There was no doubt Sienna was going to be a problem. Jase rarely talked about the sister who'd left with their mother when they were kids.

But Cole knew his friend had received a letter from his estranged mother last fall. It had pushed his recovering alcoholic father, Declan, off the wagon in a tumble that had almost cost Jase the town's mayoral election and the woman he loved.

Jase was a good man, honest and loyal. Cole understood better than most how much that meant and what a rare commodity it could be. No matter what Sienna's intentions were, her brother would give her the benefit of the doubt and open his home and heart to her. Cole wasn't convinced she deserved that chance.

Sometimes people were too kind and they got hurt because of it. His mother had been one of those gentle-hearted souls. Jase likely was, as well, although his wife, Emily, was tough enough for the both of them. Either way, Cole would do his best to protect his friend. He made his decision, called the station to tell the department's secretary his plans and got out of the car.

Sienna turned her head as he approached. She'd put on tortoise-framed sunglasses in the interim so her eyes were hidden from view. Also hidden—or at least ruthlessly tamped down—was any of the wild spirit he'd sensed in her earlier. The woman frowning up at him was so cold she could make a polar bear shiver.

"It's your lucky day, ma'am," he told her, handing back her license and registration.

Her rosy lips pressed together. "Is that so?"

"You've earned yourself a sheriff's escort."

"Was the car reported stolen?" she asked with much less concern in her voice than he would have expected. "Are you arresting me?"

"The car's fine," he answered. "For now. I'm going to make sure it stays that way. We're heading back to Aspen, Ms. Pierce, to return the Porsche."

"I don't need your help with the car."

"Good." He leaned a little closer. "Because it's not you I'm helping. It's your brother I care about."

Chapter Two

Kevin stood on the sidewalk under the hotel's blue awning, obviously arguing with one of the valets, as Sienna pulled the Porsche to the curb.

"You stole my car," he yelled as she got out, stalking toward her. "What the hell were you thinking?"

She took a moment to adjust her skirt and ran a hand through her hair, then tossed the keys to the relieved young man in the valet uniform gaping at them both.

"What were *you* thinking?" she countered, strangely empty of emotion at the moment. Her heels made a soft clicking noise on the pavement as she moved to stand in front of him.

"Come in the hotel, Sienna. We'll work this out."

"There's nothing left to work out." She reached in her purse and handed the valet a twenty-dollar bill. "Thank you," she told him with a serene smile. From the corner of her eye, she saw Cole Bennett climb out of the Jeep that had the words Crimson County Sheriff emblazoned across the side.

Under normal circumstances, Sienna loathed drawing attention to herself. Right now she couldn't find the energy to care.

"Don't be ridiculous," Kevin snapped. "I made a mistake. It was one night. I didn't even know her."

"That doesn't make it any better," Sienna said through clenched teeth.

"Ready to head out?" Cole asked as he came to stand beside her.

"Who the hell are you?" Kevin demanded.

Cole flashed an aw-shucks grin that would have done Andy Griffith proud and pointed to the badge on his chest. "Good morning to you, too, buddy. I gather you can read as well as cheat on your girlfriend?"

Kevin narrowed his eyes as he gave Cole the once-over. "A cop," he muttered.

"Sheriff," Cole corrected.

"I want this woman arrested." Kevin pointed toward Sienna. "For grand theft auto."

Sienna felt her body go rigid, then Cole put a hand on her back, whether as comfort or as a silent reminder not to flee, she couldn't tell.

"A fan of video games, I take it," Cole said conversationally. "'Grand Theft Auto' is good but I prefer 'Call of Duty' myself."

Kevin's hands clenched into fists. "This isn't a damn joke."

"I borrowed the car because I needed to compose myself," Sienna said, forcing her voice to remain calm. "Then I returned it."

"She has a witness," Cole added. He pointed to the young valet. "You saw her return it."

The gangly teen swallowed. "Yes, sir."

Kevin lifted a brow. "Come with me and work this out, and we'll let it go. Otherwise, you're going to have to explain to your parents why you were arrested for stealing a car. Mommy won't like it when that hits the news cycle, and what a blow after she just finished chemo."

He reached for her, but Cole moved forward, effectively blocking his access. "The only thing you're letting go of is Sienna," he said, all trace of civility gone from his tone. Sienna had a sudden twinge of sympathy for whatever bad guys were lurking around this section of the Rocky Mountains. Cole Bennett was clearly not a lawman to tangle with.

"This is none of your business, Sheriff."

"Are you joking?" Cole threw up his hands. "You're going to force me to use the 'I'm making it my business' line? I try not to veer into TV cop stereotypes, but if that's what it takes…"

Sienna raised a hand to her mouth, stifling a giggle. The situation was no laughing matter and Kevin had the right of it with his implied threat about her parents. Both her mom and stepdad assumed her marriage to Kevin was a done deal, the engagement just a box to check off the official wedding to-do list.

Maybe she was light-headed from lack of oxygen at this altitude, but she realized she not only had other options in life but wanted to explore them. To see who she could have become without the rigid constraints of the life her mom had orchestrated. Her mother had gone through her own emotional journey during her battle with cancer, one that had culminated with reuniting with the son she'd left behind. But Sienna wasn't on the path of reconciliation, and certainly not with Kevin.

She pointed at her ex-boyfriend. "You have a saggy butt."

The valet snickered as Kevin's mouth dropped open.

Cole turned to her, one corner of his gorgeous mouth twitching with amusement. His honey-brown gaze held hers for a moment. "You went there," he muttered. "Really?"

"I deserve better than you," she continued, moving around Cole to go toe-to-toe with Kevin. "I deserve better than how you treated me."

"Keep telling yourself that," he said, and she wondered why she'd never noticed that when he smiled it looked more like a sneer. "If you weren't such a stuffy prude, I wouldn't have had to find another woman to warm the bed. This is your—"

His head snapped back as her fist connected with his nose. She yelped, as surprised by the fact that she'd punched him as she was by the pain in her knuckles. Kevin cried out, covering his face with his hands.

"You saw her. Assault and battery," he shouted through his fingers.

"I'll keep that in mind," Cole promised. He gestured to the valet. "Get him a towel and some ice." Then he grabbed Sienna's arm. "I think you're done here."

"I didn't mean—"

"No more talking," he told her, half leading and half dragging her across the street to his Jeep. "Let's just get out of this town before you cause an even bigger scene."

She stopped a few feet from the car. "Are you going to make me sit in the back seat?"

"I should after that stunt," Cole said but opened the passenger door for her. "Get in. Your saggy bottomed ex has gone into the hotel. We should be gone by the time he comes out again."

Neither of them spoke as Cole drove out of Aspen. The upscale shops and restaurants housed in historic brick buildings gave way to apartment complexes and other, newer structures and finally changed to open meadows as he took the turn onto the highway that led to Crimson. It was the third time today she'd driven this stretch of road.

As they passed a herd of cattle grazing in a field behind a split-rail fence, Sienna searched for the mama and baby she'd spotted earlier this morning. The young calf, which couldn't have been more than a few weeks or months old, had been glued to its mother's side as if that was the safest place in the world to be.

Sienna wished she could relate to that feeling.

"I don't make scenes," she said, finally breaking the silence.

Cole's fingers tightened on the steering wheel. "Then you do a great imitation of someone who does."

"It's not my fault he cheated," she whispered.

Cole glanced over at her. "Say it like you mean it, sweetheart."

"I do. I want to." She clasped her hands tight in her lap. "He was right about one thing. My mother is going to be irked by this situation."

"The part where he cheated or the part where you broke up with him because of it?"

"We were supposed to get engaged on this trip," she said because she wasn't ready to answer his question out loud.

"Then I'd say you dodged a bullet."

She held on to that comment for a moment, cupped it between her hands—like a kid would with a firefly late on a summer night—and found she liked the light shining from it. So she tucked that light inside herself, the way she'd learned to do with anything that made her happy but would have disappointed her mother.

Sienna had learned early how to pick her battles with

Dana Crenshaw Pierce, and most of them weren't worth waging.

"Did you grow up in Crimson?" she asked, needing a break from talking about her own messed-up life.

It was a simple enough question but Cole tensed like she'd just requested he recount his first sexual encounter in graphic detail, then broadcast the story across his cruiser's radio.

"No."

"Somewhere in Colorado?"

"No."

"Okay then." When he didn't add anything more, she threw up her hands. "I'm going to assume you're some sort of super secret law enforcement guy and you've had your past wiped out by the covert government agency that basically owns you and if you breathe one word of where you came from or who you used to be, everyone in your family will die."

"They're already dead," he said quietly.

"Oh." She reached out a hand, placed it on his arm. "I'm sorry."

He swerved off the highway to the shoulder, braking hard. The Jeep's tires crunched in the dirt and gravel. Sienna tried to catch her breath as she was jostled in her seat.

"Let's get a few things straight." Cole's voice was as jarring as fingernails on a chalkboard. "I don't need or want your pity."

"I wasn't—" she began, but he held up a hand.

"We're not friends," he continued. "We're not *going* to be friends. You were a mess this morning and I was taking care of my friend by taking care of you. If the ex-boyfriend is any indication, you need serious help with your taste in men. Maybe you need help in general." He jabbed a finger toward her, then back at himself. "I'm not going to be the one to give it. I'm dropping you off at the rental car agency, and we're done. Is that clear?"

"Crystal," she said, feeling as if she had ice forming inside her veins. She straightened her skirt, wishing it were a few inches longer so her legs weren't exposed to Cole's gaze. She could feel him watching her, although she refused to make eye contact.

She sat tall, shoulders back, her posture impeccable— the way she'd been taught in the five years of ballet classes her mother had wrenched out of her after Dana had married Craig Pierce and had the money to reinvent herself. To recreate both of their lives—a do-over of monumental proportions and one Sienna had never wanted.

Eventually Cole blew out a long breath, then started driving again. Sienna didn't so much as twitch until he pulled into a rental car parking lot that was part of a strip mall a mile past the Crimson city limits sign. The rental car place shared the space with a grocery store, a hair salon and a sandwich shop.

As soon as the Jeep stopped, she unfastened her seat belt and opened the door.

"Thank you for the ride," she mumbled over her shoulder, because along with perfect posture, good manners had been drilled into her. Oddly, she felt almost as angry with Cole as she was with Kevin, which was stupid because the sheriff didn't owe her anything. He'd done her a favor this morning, but they weren't friends. He was nothing to her, so why had her chest ached when he'd told her exactly that?

"Sienna." He reached for her arm but she shrugged away from his touch.

"We're done, Sheriff." He winced slightly, as if he

didn't appreciate having his words thrown back at him. "I can handle things from here."

She slammed the door shut and walked toward the building, telling herself she was glad to be leaving behind Sheriff Cole Bennett and this whole humiliating morning.

Fifteen minutes later, Cole pushed through the door of the mayor's office on the second floor of the county courthouse. "Where's Jase? He's not answering his phone."

"Good morning to you, too." Emily Crenshaw inclined her head, then turned her attention to the computer screen. "Help yourself to fresh coffee. Not sure what's got your boxers in a bunch today." Her gaze flicked back to him. "Or is it boxer briefs? You look like a boxer brief type of guy, Sheriff. Definitely not tighty-whities, something for which we can all be grateful."

"Emily."

"Either way, grab a cup of coffee, then come back and I'll give you a do-over on this conversation." She lifted a brow. "I learned that trick from my job at the front desk of the elementary school. Some kids need help learning how to appropriately greet people. I guess you didn't get that lesson or you've forgotten." She flashed a wide smile. "I'm here to help."

Cole felt his mouth drop open and quickly closed it again. What was it about this day and sassy blondes? But Emily Crenshaw was a force to be reckoned with and currently sat in the computer chair normally occupied by Jase's sweet-tempered secretary, Molly.

Cole was developing a new appreciation for sweet-tempered.

He grabbed a mug from the cart positioned along the far wall and poured himself a steaming cup of coffee. "Good morning, Emily," he said as he took a drink. "You're filling in for Molly today?"

"Just for the morning." Emily pushed away from the computer and smiled. "She had to take her mom to a doctor's appointment, and Davey is in a Lego camp this week. It's always a challenge to keep a first-grade boy occupied during the summer."

"I can imagine," he said even as he thought of how he and his brother, Shep, had run wild through the various army bases around the world where his dad had been stationed back in the day.

"Thank you for the pleasantries," Emily told him. "Jase had a meeting with the city finance director, so I doubt his phone is on. They're on the first floor, so he should be back soon."

"I'll wait."

"What's going on, Cole?" Emily's big eyes narrowed. She looked a little bit like Sienna, now that he thought about it. Blond hair, blue eyes, beautiful with that certain shine that time spent in a big city gave to women. Sienna was a couple inches taller, her face more heart-shaped with delicate features.

Emily was a Crimson native who'd moved away, then back with her young son early last year. She was different from Sienna in one major way—Emily radiated happiness. It had been hard earned, he knew, and was glad that she and Jase had worked out their issues.

She stood, and he was reminded of another significant difference between the two women. Emily was seven months pregnant, which made her seem somehow more intimidating than usual. Give Cole a bar fight to break up or even an underground drug bust rather than be stared down by a heavily pregnant woman.

He shrugged and gave her his don't-mess-with-me

law enforcement face. "I need to talk to him. Sheriff's office business."

She crossed her arms over her chest, resting them on her round belly. "Do I look stupid?"

So much for intimidation. "Um...no."

"It seems like somebody's in trouble with my better half."

Cole turned, profoundly grateful to see Jase Crenshaw standing in the door to the outer office, one side of his mouth curved as he looked between Cole and Emily.

"The sheriff wants to talk to you," Emily told her husband.

"Okay," Jase answered and walked forward, leaning over the receptionist desk to kiss her, while gently placing a hand on her baby bump.

Cole quickly turned and refilled his coffee mug, uncomfortable with the easy show of affection.

"But he's acting suspicious." Emily frowned at Cole. "Something's up and I want to know what it is."

"It's nothing," Cole insisted and flicked a help-me glance to Jase.

"You might as well say it." Jase shrugged. "If she doesn't find out now, I'll have to tell her later."

"What if it's confidential?"

Emily sniffed. "I'm his *wife*. He tells me everything."

Jase nodded. "It's true. I'm not an expert on marriage, but I do understand that honesty is a pretty important foundation."

Anger spiked in Cole's chest, familiar to him as his face in the mirror. Not at Jase or Emily but at memories of his own father's lies and deceptions—the ones that had torn apart his family.

He blew out a breath, forcing his emotions under control. "I clocked a woman driving twenty miles over the speed limit coming into Crimson this morning."

"An out-of-towner, I assume?" Jase asked.

Emily scrunched up her nose. "What does that have to do—?"

"Her name was Sienna Pierce," Cole interrupted.

Emily immediately placed a hand on Jase's arm, almost the same way Sienna had done with Cole in the car earlier. He'd overreacted to the gesture but couldn't seem to stop himself from freaking out any time he was forced to talk about his family.

It was one of the reasons he'd first applied as a sheriff's deputy in Crimson five years ago. No one knew him here and it was easy to keep his conversations about his past vague—just the way he liked it.

"You gave my sister a speeding ticket?" Jase asked, his tone almost unnaturally calm.

"Not exactly," Cole answered. He'd planned to share with Jase the details of his morning run-in with Sienna but now the words wouldn't come. As reserved as she pretended to be, he knew Sienna had been humiliated by her cheating ex-boyfriend. He doubted that was information she'd appreciate being used as her calling card in Crimson. "More like a warning."

Emily raised a brow at Cole as her hand tightened on Jase's arm. "Is that what this is?"

"I thought you'd want to know she was here," Cole told his friend. "I got the impression she hadn't called first."

"Hardly," Jase said with a small laugh. "I haven't talked to Sienna since the night my mom drove away with her."

"Because she refused to see you when you visited your mom last Christmas." Emily came around the desk and laced her fingers through Jase's. "She made it clear she wanted nothing to do with you."

"I wonder what changed," Jase murmured, almost under his breath.

Her whole world from the looks of it, Cole wanted to answer. It's what he should have shared. But instead he only shrugged. "I don't know her plans but thought you'd want to know, and your dad…"

Jase groaned. "This is going to rock his world."

"She has no business showing up out of the blue." Emily reminded Cole of an Amazon warrior getting ready for battle or a grizzly mama standing between a pack of coyotes and one of her cubs. "If she upsets Declan—"

"I'll take care of it." Jase wrapped an arm around her shoulder. "Don't get riled up, Em."

Emily only rolled her eyes. "I love you, Jase Crenshaw, but you know me better than that. Telling me not to get riled up is like telling a retriever not to fetch the ball."

Cole laughed, then tried to cover it with a cough when Emily gave him one of her looks. "Sorry," he mumbled. "But you compared yourself to a dog."

"No more free coffee for you," she said, but her lips twitched as she said it.

"Thank you, Cole," Jase said. "I appreciate the heads-up."

"You bet. I've got to check in at the station. Call if you need anything."

He placed his mug on the cart and walked out of the office, rubbing a hand over his jaw as he stepped into the warm June sunshine. Several people waved and Cole forced himself to smile and greet them in return, even though the sick pit in his stomach was growing wider by the second.

He didn't owe Sienna Pierce a thing. So why did he feel like she was the one who needed protecting in Crimson? Jase had Emily and his dad and the whole town in his corner. From what he could tell, Sienna had no one.

Cole could relate, and the strange connection he'd felt to her this morning had somehow taken root inside him and refused to let go.

Ten kinds of trouble, he'd told her, but wondered if he'd underestimated even that.

Chapter Three

Sienna stared at the house tucked amid the pine trees, then checked the GPS on her phone one more time. She'd made a reservation at The Bumblebee Bed and Breakfast at 1 Ivy Lane on a whim after picking up an adorable business card at the counter of the grocery store next to the rental car agency.

Normally Sienna stuck to luxury hotel chains. She gravitated toward sleek decor and modern conveniences. But something about the colorful flowers and cheerful bees drawn on the card appealed to her. She needed some color and cheer in her life.

But she also wanted a hot shower and a toilet that flushed. Nothing about the plumbing van sitting in the driveway of the dilapidated house at the end of the long, winding drive gave her confidence she'd find either at The Bumblebee.

If her mother were here, she would have been happy

to enumerate the ways Sienna had managed to mess up her life—all of them in one day. Dana Pierce loved making lists.

The only thing on Sienna's to-do list right now was getting back in the compact car she'd rented and finding a decent hotel.

"Sienna!"

She turned back toward the house, surprised to hear her name shouted out like a long-lost friend had just spotted her.

"You're Sienna, right?" A tiny pixie of a woman ran toward her, appearing from the trees like a woodland sprite. "I've been waiting for you." The woman stopped, clasped a hand over her mouth. "Scratch that last part. It sounds like the start of some creepy horror movie." She waved her hands in the air as dark curls bounced around her face. "I've been waiting for you," she repeated in a deep, melodramatic voice. "You know what I mean, though. I'm excited you found us…me, rather…The Bumblebee, that is."

"You must be Paige," Sienna said, reaching out a hand.

"Who else?" the woman asked, bypassing her outstretched hand to give Sienna a tight hug. The innkeeper might be small, but she was strong, practically squeezing all the air out of Sienna's lungs. "You're my first guest. We're going to have the best week."

"This isn't summer camp," Sienna said quietly, making Paige laugh.

"I know, silly. But I just got the sign up today." She pointed behind her to a hand-painted piece of cardboard that read The Bumblebee B&B. It leaned against the edge of the porch rail. "Not quite up," Paige admitted. "But you still found me." She scrunched her winged brows, emerald green eyes zeroing in on Sienna. "How did you find me anyway?"

"The business cards you left at the grocery."

"I remember now." Paige nodded. "I picked them up from the post office on my way to buy food for dinner. I told Rodney—he's the manager at the Shop & Go—not to put them out until next week."

"Apparently he did anyway."

Paige squeezed Sienna's arms like they were best friends. "Lucky for both of us."

"Are you sure?" Sienna inclined her head toward the plumbing truck in the driveway, then pointed to the various pieces of furniture sitting in the front yard. "It looks like you might need a bit more time to get ready."

Paige gave her a brilliant smile. "I'm as ready as I'll ever be."

Terrifying, Sienna thought to herself.

"Then why the plumber?"

"A leak in the first-floor bathroom," Paige said, spacing her first finger and thumb a tiny width apart as she held them up to her eye. "But your bedroom is upstairs."

"That's good."

"Only now," Paige said, wrinkling her nose, "I'll be sharing it because mine is downstairs."

"Not so good." Although Sienna had a brother right here in Crimson, most of her life she'd been an only child. Her mother liked to tell her she wasn't good at sharing, and Sienna had no reason not to believe it because she'd never had to.

"It will only be for a day or two." Paige flashed a bright smile that only wavered slightly. "Maybe."

"I don't mind finding a normal—I mean regular—hotel in town."

"Good luck with that. The rodeo's at the county fairgrounds this weekend. Everything's booked from here to Grand Junction. Unless you want to stay in Aspen."

Sienna shook her head. "I don't."

"Huh. No offense, but you look like the Aspen type. Other than the mustard stain on your blouse."

"Why would I take offense to that?" Sienna picked at the dried mustard on the front of her shirt.

"Did you get a hot dog at the Shop & Go?" Paige asked instead of answering the question. "They're yummy."

"It was tasty," Sienna admitted. The hot dog had been the best thing she'd eaten in ages. Normally she stuck to a high protein, low-carb, all organic and very little fun diet. The hot dog had been another small act in the process of reclaiming her life. Or claiming it for the first time, since it had never truly felt like hers.

"Do you have luggage?"

"Yes, but not here." Sienna had left her suitcase with the hotel's bellman in Aspen this morning. She supposed it was still there and figured she'd have to drive back over at some point to retrieve it. But she wasn't ready for another potential confrontation with Kevin. "I picked up toiletries at the grocery store."

"I can lend you some clothes."

"That would be interesting." Paige was at least four inches shorter than Sienna and curvy like some throwback pinup girl from the forties. "Since you're new at this whole innkeeper thing, I should tell you that in normal circumstances you wouldn't offer your clothes to a paying guest."

"Not to assume too much," Paige said, inclining her head, "but do you think these are normal circumstances for either of us?"

Sienna blew out a breath. "No."

"Please stay," Paige said, then gave a nervous laugh.

"That sounded desperate. I don't mean it like that." She laughed again. "Except I sort of do. This was my grandma's house." She gestured to the ramshackle but still charming lodge with faded rough-sawed logs notched together and deep green shutters bordering the windows on the front. "My mom inherited it when Grammy died last year, and I convinced her to let me get it up and running again."

"I'm sorry for your loss," Sienna said automatically.

"Thank you," Paige whispered. "It's beautiful out here...but also quiet."

Sienna nodded, looking around the cul-de-sac. There were a few houses at the top of the street, where she'd turned onto Ivy Lane, but The Bumblebee's property was clearly the largest and most private.

"Grammy had five acres," Paige said, as if reading her thoughts. "It borders the old ski resort in back. We even have a view of the main chairlift. It hasn't operated for years, although some developer bought the property recently. My grandma fought like crazy with the old owner about selling this place and making it part of the resort. I'm hoping the new owner will be more friendly and that The Bumblebee will be in the right place to cater to skiers or families vacationing in Crimson."

"Smart move," Sienna murmured.

Paige beamed at her. "Thank you for saying that. My family thinks I'm crazy. I'm not exactly following the path they expected me to take."

There was something in the woman's gaze—a combination of hope and fear with a healthy dose of uncertainty and pride mixed in—that Sienna imagined she might see in her own eyes when she looked in the mirror.

"I'll stay," she said. If Sienna was going to forge her own way in life, she had to start taking some risks in order to figure out what she wanted that life to be. Somewhere between Kevin's butt and the ride in Cole's Jeep, she'd decided the time had come to take charge of her life on her own terms.

And Colorado, far away from her mother, seemed like a better place to spread her wings than in Chicago, tethered by the constraints of her regular life. Maybe she'd actually forge a relationship with her dad and brother instead of the awkward face-offs she imagined. The thought made panic spike in her belly, and she pressed a hand to her stomach. One step at a time.

Whether a risk or an adventure, coming to Crimson as the inaugural guest at The Bumblebee B&B seemed like the right move on her new journey. It would be interesting to see where it took her.

"One more refill."

Sienna grabbed the red plastic cup from Paige's hand and filled it to the brim.

"Too much." Paige grimaced, shaking her head. "You could put a Russian under the table with the amount of vodka in that."

"It's mainly lemonade," Sienna argued, then hiccuped. "I swear."

Paige rolled her eyes but took a sip. "It's good."

"Told you so." Sienna took a long drink from her cup. "An added bonus is that it makes this place look a lot better."

"True," Paige agreed and both women turned from the long butcher-block island in the kitchen to survey the house.

The kitchen opened onto a cozy family room in which all the furniture was shoved up against one wall. Half the wood floor had been ripped up after the plumber found a slow leak that had caused damage to the foundation. The

Bumblebee's minor plumbing project now looked like it would stretch out at least a week, if not longer.

Paige had immediately started hyperventilating when she'd been given the news this afternoon. Sienna had shoved the novice innkeeper into a chair, found a paper bag for her to breathe into, then gotten a contractor recommendation from the plumber.

"You're the guest," Paige had said, wheezing into the bag. "You shouldn't be—"

"I'll manage," Sienna assured her. Besides, the more she focused on Paige's problems, the less time she had to think about her real reason for this impulsive trip to Crimson—confronting her dad after twenty years of no contact between them.

Plumbing issues were way less trouble than family drama.

Once Paige had calmed down, she'd insisted on making dinner, which consisted of an array of surprisingly delicious frozen appetizers heated in the oven. Sienna had searched through the cabinets until she'd found a decent bottle of vodka.

"Grammy liked a little nip before bed," Paige explained.

Sienna had concocted a hard lemonade drink, and no matter how much vodka she added it still seemed to go down far too easily.

They'd watched a few episodes of a reality TV show about pampered pets, then Paige had pulled a disco ball strobe light out of a closet.

"Dance party!" she'd shouted and Sienna had been too blissfully numb to argue.

They'd danced for what seemed like hours, avoiding the caution tape that roped off the hole in the floor. When Sienna realized she was a sweaty and thirsty mess, she made another pitcher of hard lemonade. She smiled as she watched the bright flashes of color on the bumblebee wallpaper in the kitchen.

"This has been the funnest night ever," Paige said, then yawned.

"Ever," Sienna agreed without hesitation. She'd never had a night like this, one filled with laughing and dancing and ignoring all of her worries. Paige had asked a few subtle questions about what brought Sienna to Crimson but hadn't seemed to mind Sienna's vague answers.

Both women jumped when a loud knock sounded on the front door.

"Stupid neighbors," Paige muttered, stumbling a little as she hopped off her stool. "I bet they called the cops again."

"The cops?"

"The grumpy couple down the street has the local department on speed dial. If I so much as put my trash out too early, they report me. I'm guessing they think colored lights from a disco ball are the devil's handiwork."

A sinking pit opened in Sienna's stomach. It was highly unlikely Cole would be the one to respond to a call like this but with the way her luck was running...

"I'm going to head upsta—"

She got up from her stool just as Paige turned toward her. Sienna's arm jostled the cup Paige held, and vodka lemonade splashed all over the front of Paige's pajamas.

"Yuck," Paige cried. "I'm going to be a sticky mess. You get the door while I change."

"I can't—"

Paige's eyes widened. "Don't make me answer it when I'm practically bathed in vodka. A plumbing problem is bad enough. Who wants to stay at a B&B where the lady who runs it is a stinking drunk?"

The knock sounded again, more forcefully this time.

"It's not like potential guests will hear about it," Sienna protested, shaking her head.

"This is Crimson." Paige threw up her hands. "Everyone will know." She made a kissing sound toward Sienna. "I'll be back in a jiffy."

Sienna sighed as Paige disappeared into her bedroom. She turned down the music, flipped off the disco light and padded to the door, trying to ignore both her hammering heart and the fact that she was wearing a set of Paige's tie-dyed pajamas.

She wet her lips with her tongue, said a silent prayer that some low-level officer had gotten stuck with this call and opened the door.

Cole Bennett stood on the other side.

Chapter Four

"Seriously?"

Sienna's blue eyes burned like the center of a flame as she glared at him.

"The neighbors called," he said, like he owed her some sort of explanation. "Mrs. Morrison saw lights flashing through the trees while she was walking her dog before bed tonight. She was convinced they were a result of some sort of unlawful activity."

"I heard about the neighbors," Sienna muttered. "Paige and I were having a dance party." She glowered at him like he'd put the older couple up to making the complaint. As if he didn't have anything better to do than show up to check out the situation—like he'd been looking for an excuse to see her again. The latter might be slightly true, even though he'd never admit it.

"Don't you have deputies or something?" she demanded, crossing her arms over the faded tie-dyed tank top she wore. She had matching pajama pants, and with her blond hair tumbling over her shoulders and the pink glow to her cheeks, she was even more beautiful now than she'd been earlier that morning.

"I wanted to check on you." The fact that he admitted it obviously surprised her as much as it did him.

"How did you know I was here?"

She moved back and he stepped into the house, gently closing the ancient screen door behind him. He didn't bother with the front door. It was a perfect Colorado night, about ten degrees cooler than it had been when the sun was out, and Cole needed the fresh air to remind him to keep his self-control in place.

"Rodney mentioned you picked up one of the business cards for The Bumblebee. There aren't many open rooms in town because of the rodeo, so I assumed this is where you ended up. Once the call came in, I had no doubt you were here." He inclined his head. "You and trouble and all that."

"I don't get into trouble," she insisted, narrowing her eyes.

"Other than speeding and stealing a car and—"

"I didn't steal the car."

"You stole a car?"

Cole looked up as Paige Harper rushed into the room. "That's crazy in an awesome *Thelma and Louise* kind of way. Hey, Sheriff."

"Evening, Paige."

"Sorry about the music."

"It was more the lights this time. They worried Mrs. Morrison."

"Of course they did. She's probably jealous that she has no reason to turn on disco lights." Paige nudged Sienna. "If you want to be Thelma, I can be Louise. Or we can trade roles. I'm more of a Thelma anyway, I think. Sheriff, do you have an opinion on that?"

"Uh, no," Cole admitted, not sure what the bubbly innkeeper was talking about. But it didn't matter because he saw the start of a smile curve Sienna's full mouth and felt suddenly grateful for Paige Harper and her ramshackle inn.

Even though she seemed tough, he had a feeling Sienna was more vulnerable in Crimson than she'd ever let on. If Jase's wariness and Emily's underlying temper were any indication, she might need a friend during her time in town. Paige would be the perfect ally.

"I'm not Thelma *or* Louise," Sienna said. "I borrowed a car from my ex-boyfriend this morning and then I returned it. The sheriff was a witness. I'm not planning on causing trouble. Pierce women don't *do* trouble."

"You're a Crenshaw here in Crimson," Cole felt compelled to point out. "And the Crenshaw family has a long history of trouble in this town."

"Jase Crenshaw is the family you're in town to visit?" Paige asked, wide-eyed.

Sienna nodded tightly. "Jase and my dad."

"Why didn't you say so in the first place? Jase is a great guy. I'm new enough to Crimson that I don't know much about anyone's past history, but I can almost guarantee Jase isn't involved in any kind of trouble. He's too good for that."

"How do you know my brother?" Sienna asked quietly, shifting away from Paige and closer to Cole. He had the ridiculous urge to wrap an arm around her shoulder but managed to keep his hands at his sides.

"Well, he's the mayor so everyone knows him. But I met him personally at a town council meeting when I first started working on The Bumblebee. He was really helpful and supportive of my ideas for the inn. Everyone in Crimson loves Jase."

"Of course they do." Sienna's shoulders sagged.

Cole realized she had no reason to know that her brother was the town's favorite son. Jase had been through plenty—overcoming his family's less-than-stellar reputation and taking care of his father during the years Declan couldn't pull himself out of the bottle. But now Jase was universally liked and well respected, both in Crimson and throughout the network of high-country towns in this part of Colorado.

Cole wasn't sure why this knowledge seemed to affect Sienna like the sharp point of a pin to a balloon, but he could almost see her deflating before his eyes.

"You should invite Jase and Emily to the inn for dinner. They can bring Davey, too. He's a sweet kid."

"Davey?"

"Emily's son," Paige clarified. "You haven't met him?"

Sienna shook her head.

"What about Emily?"

"His wife?" Sienna asked Cole.

"They got married last year," he confirmed.

Sienna looked at Paige again. "Jase and I aren't exactly close."

"When was the last time you saw him?"

"Um...about twenty years ago."

Paige whistled softly. "We're going to need more vodka for this story."

"No more vodka," Cole said at the same time as Sienna.

"Or disco lights," Cole added, pointing at each of the women.

Paige pressed two fingers to her forehead. "Probably a good idea. I can already feel a headache brewing. I'm going to go to bed. Sienna, you can give me the fascinating details of your family history over coffee and muffins in the morning."

"There's nothing fascinating about me."

Paige darted a glance toward Cole, as if she knew he wanted to argue.

"I'll get going then," he said instead. "Keep the music down and pull the shades if you want to turn on the disco lights."

"Sienna will walk you to your car," Paige offered. "'Night, you two." She turned, then looked back over her shoulder. "By the way, there's something fascinating about everyone. Some of us just need to figure out what it is."

"Let's go," Sienna said, starting to move past him.

He placed a hand on her arm, not surprised to find her skin hot to the touch. As much as he might want to deny it, it seemed neither of them could ignore the flame of attraction that burned between them. "You don't need to walk me."

"Come on, Sheriff," she answered, shrugging off his touch.

He followed her onto the porch, the light above the doorframe casting a pale glow. He was used to people calling him Sheriff, and normally he liked it. At times his job felt like the only thing that defined him. But coming from Sienna, the word was wrong. He wanted to hear his name on her lips, preferably whispered over and over as he drove her crazy with desire.

No doubt he should have had a deputy answer this call tonight.

"I'm guessing you didn't contact Jase or Declan yet," he said into the silence.

She grabbed the porch railing, as if to steady herself— a result of the alcohol or the mention of her dad and brother, he couldn't tell which. "I wanted a day to get settled. Today wasn't exactly filled with shining star moments for me."

"Except maybe a pajama dance party. That's the stuff of shining moments, not to mention male fantasies everywhere."

She laughed softly, and once again he felt it all the way to his toes. The sound was low and husky, like she was as out of practice with laughter as he was. Holding out her arms, she spun in a small circle on the gravel driveway. "This outfit isn't the stuff of anyone's fantasy."

"You have no idea."

"How long have you lived in Crimson?" she asked suddenly, a variation of the line of questioning he'd reacted to so badly earlier.

He wanted to keep it together tonight. They'd made it to his Jeep, the Crimson County Sheriff's emblem emblazoned across the side and illuminated in the moonlight.

"I came here a few years back for a deputy position. There were some shake-ups within the department and Jase convinced me to run for sheriff in the last election. That was two years ago."

"You and Jase are close," she whispered.

"Yeah. Your brother is a good man, Sienna."

"My brother," she repeated as if she couldn't quite grasp the meaning of the word, then turned so she was facing Cole. "Did you tell him I was here?"

"Yes."

She sucked her bottom lip into her mouth and bit down. Cole's knees went weak.

"I should probably leave in the morning. Coming to Crimson seemed like a great idea when I was all fired up this morning, but now—"

"Don't go." He reached out, tucked a stray lock of hair behind her ear.

"I can't believe Jase would want me here. He came to visit our mom last winter. I wasn't exactly…cordial."

"Emily mentioned that."

"The wife. Is she going to be a problem for me?"

"Emily is protective of Jase. He's sometimes too nice for his own good. His dad…your dad has needed a lot of caregiving through the years. There were some dark days, most of them before I got to town, but Declan has stumbled even recently. Sobriety is a harsh mistress for him sometimes."

"I remember the drinking." Her eyes closed, and he watched her chest rise and fall as she sucked in a deep breath. "I don't remember much, maybe because that's the way Mom wanted it. We barely spoke about Jase or my dad once we left Crimson. But the smell of whiskey brings back snippets of memory. Most of them I should probably forget. My parents weren't exactly kind to each other when they drank."

"That's fairly common. Alcohol doesn't bring out the best in anyone."

She blinked, her blue eyes clear as a mountain lake as she looked up at him. "My mom hasn't taken a drink, not even a sip of champagne at a wedding, since she left here. Even though she wouldn't talk about it, I always got the impression she blamed the town for her downward spiral as much as she did my dad."

"I'm sorry she had to break ties with Colorado so dramatically, but this town isn't to blame for the troubles she had. It's a great community."

"You're the sheriff," she said with a smile. "Of course

you think that. Everyone has to be nice to you. They'll end up in jail otherwise."

He laughed. "Not exactly."

"Do you have a girlfriend, Sheriff?"

Cole, he wanted to shout, suddenly desperate to hear her say his name.

"Nope. Work keeps me too busy."

"Lame excuse. I bet there is a line of women hoping you'll notice them."

"Hardly."

"How many times a week does some generous citizen…" She leaned in closer and he caught the light floral scent of her shampoo. "Some *female* citizen," she clarified, "bring fresh muffins by your office?"

"Only on Fridays," he admitted, then shrugged when Sienna looked confused. "Our office manager went low-carb last year. Marlene limits the baked goods to once a week."

Sienna shook her head, another smile playing around the corners of her mouth. "My mom only referred to Crimson as 'that place,' but I always imagined it as some sort of high-altitude version of Sodom and Gomorrah." Her smile widened. "It's more like mountain Mayberry."

"I'm not Andy Griffith," Cole argued, annoyed by the implied comparison.

"If you start whistling—"

He leaned in and kissed her, somehow wanting to prove that he wasn't the easygoing, small-town lawman she presumed him to be. At least that's the reason he gave himself. The truth was he couldn't resist her one more second. Her smart mouth and sassy attitude. All the ways she tried to pretend she wasn't hurting.

The fact that he recognized the loneliness in her gaze

because he saw the same thing in his own eyes every time he looked in the mirror.

She stilled for a moment, then sighed and sank into the kiss. It wasn't the reaction he'd expected and the surprise of it made his body burn. He'd figured she would snap at him or give him a swift punch to the gut. But she seemed to need the touch as much as he did.

He moved closer, still touching her with only his mouth, but close enough that he could feel her heat. Her mouth was soft under his, sweet and pliant. She made another sound, a soft moan, and swayed closer. Cole reached out a hand and gently gripped the graceful column of her neck.

The contact was enough to break the spell between them. Sienna stepped back, away from his grasp, her fingertips pressing against her swollen lips.

"Why did you do that?" She seemed more confused than angry, which was a small victory in Cole's mind.

"I needed to know if your mouth was as soft as it looks."

She gathered her long blond hair and flipped it over her shoulder, rolling her eyes at him. "I don't think I've ever been described as soft."

"You're soft," he assured her. "At least when you're not being disagreeable and argumentative."

"I don't argue and I can be agreeable when I want to." She no longer looked dazed. Instead the spark had returned to her gaze. He liked it there. "I don't need to prove anything to anyone."

He shrugged. "Except maybe yourself."

"You shouldn't kiss me again."

"Do you want to argue about it?"

She narrowed her eyes. "Good night, Sheriff."

"Call me Cole," he said, unable to stop himself from making the request.

She stared at him so long he wasn't sure she'd answer, then whispered, "Good night, Cole," and turned for the house.

He watched her walk away until the front door clicked shut behind her. Crickets chirped from the bushes and an owl in a tree at the edge of the forest gave a mournful hoot.

Cole had come to Colorado as an escape, running from the scandal and tragedy that surrounded his parents' deaths.

He'd found refuge in small-town life and in serving and protecting the people who made this town their home. But he wasn't a part of the fabric of Crimson's community in the same way as Jase. Growing up an army brat, Cole had become an expert at making connections without truly allowing himself to bond to anyone or anything. Hell, he'd never even owned a dog, which was practically a requirement in Colorado.

Sienna made him feel different. Maybe because she was also so obviously alone. He could allow himself this connection with her—but whether it was real or imagined he couldn't quite say.

Did it really matter? Cole knew that along with emotional ties came the very real possibility of someone getting hurt. He'd had a ringside seat to watch his mom unravel after his father's death until her heart had literally given out. He didn't want any part of that kind of pain, either for himself or anyone around him.

Marlene down at the department liked to tease him about the parade of women who made excuses to stop in. But Cole wasn't interested in getting close to a woman, even to an almost irresistible blonde who took his breath away every time he looked at her.

At least that's what he tried to convince himself of

as he climbed in his truck and drove through the quiet streets of the town he'd made his home. Attraction was one thing, but he wouldn't let it go any further.

Chapter Five

Sienna couldn't have said how long she'd been sitting in her rental car outside the tiny brick duplex the next morning, but her backside was numb and her throat had gone dry from the air conditioner blowing through the vents in the dash.

She'd turned the car on and off at least a dozen times, psyching herself up for approaching the modest home. Within those walls lived a man she hadn't seen in two decades but who was never far from her mind, no matter how hard she tried to forget him.

A knock on the driver's side window made her jerk around so fast she banged her forehead into the glass. She let out a sound somewhere between a scream and a groan, blinking away tears of fear, frustration and pain. Her gaze focused on the gray-haired man standing next to the car, and her stomach dipped.

The years hadn't been kind to Declan Crenshaw, but

Sienna knew the signs of age had as much to do with the choices he'd made as the passage of time.

She looked at him through the glass, half tempted to throw the car into Drive and speed away from everything this moment represented.

For his part, her dad looked like he could wait all day for her to decide whether to acknowledge him. It was that air of serene patience that made her punch down the window button.

"I thought you might run out of gas idling at the curb so long," he said conversationally.

"It seemed like a good idea to sneak up on me?" she shot back, pressing her fingers to the goose egg quickly rising on her forehead.

He ran a hand over his face, where at least a day of salt-and-pepper whiskers shadowed his jaw. "Figured you'd drive off if I came at you through the front door."

She wouldn't tell him he'd been right. There was no way she'd admit that he had any sort of insight into her behavior. "You don't seem surprised to see me."

"Jase called yesterday." He inclined his head. "Damn, you look like your mother."

"So I'm told."

"You have softer features, though. And straighter hair."

Sienna huffed out a small laugh. It was the second time in less than twenty-four hours she'd been described as soft, after a lifetime becoming reconciled to her hard edges.

"How's your mother doing?"

"You can't expect me to answer that," she said, not bothering to hide the snap in her tone. No matter the issues Sienna had with her mom, Dana was the one who'd chosen her at least. She owed her mother some loyalty.

Declan stared, as if weighing her answer...as if weighing her. Then he asked, "How are you?"

He had no right to know anything about her life after all these years. Except she was the one who'd sought him out.

Sienna and her mother had left Crimson years ago, and not once had her father contacted her. He hadn't so much as sent a birthday card. How was she ever supposed to put aside the pain of rejection that was woven into every inch of the woman she'd become?

"I can't do this," she whispered, glancing up at him.

Something flashed in his blue eyes, but he didn't argue. There was no fight, no begging her to stay. He simply stepped back from the car as she rolled up the window, and watched her drive away.

Tears streamed down her face as she turned the corner. Had she really expected him to fight for her? Did her arrival in town mean anything to him? Jase had told him she'd come to Crimson, but neither man had sought her out. They had their lives here, and Sienna had stopped being a part of them a long time ago.

Why should that change now? Growing up without a real father might have defined her, but it clearly had very little impact on the man who'd let her go.

When her vision blurred to the point she couldn't see the road in front of her, she pulled off to the side, jolting as the car's tire scraped the edge of the curb. Where had these tears come from? Declan Crenshaw wasn't worth crying over—that's what her mother would say.

She took several deep breaths, took a wad of napkins from the glove compartment and wiped her face. Grabbing her cell phone from the passenger side seat, she punched in a number and hit the speaker button.

"You've been avoiding my calls." Her mother's crisp tone fairly dripped with censure.

"I have bad service up here," Sienna lied and heard

Dana's disapproving tsk across the miles. Felt the subtle reprimand to her core.

"Kevin spoke with your father this morning. He mentioned you had a spat."

"It was more than a *spat*." Sienna drummed her fingers against the steering wheel. "I broke up with him."

A soft hiss from Dana.

"I found him in bed with another woman," Sienna added before her mother could tell her she was making a mistake.

"These things happen," Dana said quietly, her lack of emotion communicating far too much for Sienna's taste. "You'd do well to give him a bit of warning when he isn't expecting you."

"You can't be serious," Sienna said through her teeth before remembering that her mother was always serious. "He cheated on me and somehow it's my fault because I surprised him at the hotel?"

"I didn't say that," Dana insisted in her usual measured tone. "Not exactly. Kevin is important to your father's business, Sienna. Especially with him heading up the merger. You know it's scheduled to go through in a month. He can't afford to have you disrupting the status quo. Remember your place."

"My place." Sienna raised a hand to her head, pressing fingertips against the bump there and trying to pretend that the headache was the reason she felt like crying again. "Craig Pierce isn't my father, Mom. Let's not act like—"

"He raised you from the time you were a girl."

"He tolerated me because he wanted you," Sienna clarified. There had never been any question as to her value with her stepfather. Mostly she hadn't minded. Dana had made sure she understood they were to be grateful for

Craig's largesse and the opportunities being part of the powerful Pierce family opened to them.

"You never wanted for anything," Dana insisted, the words coming out fast and with traces of the Alabama accent she'd tried so hard to erase. As far as Dana was concerned, she didn't have any past before meeting Craig Pierce. It was as if she'd been sprung fully formed as a society wife out of the mold Craig created.

But Sienna remembered the months before her mother had met Craig, when she'd managed to secure a job as a hostess in one of the toniest restaurants in Chicago. It was the type of stuffy, wood-paneled spot where local businessmen came for power lunches and drinks after work. Dana had spent hours with old magazines and CDs she'd borrowed from the library, studying Jackie Kennedy and Grace Kelly, modeling her appearance, the way she dressed and even her mode of speaking after the two women.

Within weeks, all traces of Dana Crenshaw, hard-living party girl had been wiped away. Sienna remembered being mesmerized by her mother's transformation. Back in Crimson, she'd always been vaguely embarrassed by her parents—Declan and Dana were too loud, hanging all over each other when they weren't fighting in a way most parents didn't. Plus they'd lived in the shabbiest trailer in the trailer park, when Sienna's classmates came from town or the outlying ranches around Crimson.

So it had been true that she'd never wanted for anything material once her mother met and quickly married Craig. But love and acceptance were another story, one Dana had shoved onto a high shelf to gather dust in the pristine mansion they'd moved into with Craig. Out of necessity, Sienna had quickly forced herself to forget where she'd come from and anything else but that gratitude she was meant to feel for her new life.

"I saw him today," she said suddenly.

From her mother's sharp intake of breath, she knew Dana understood whom she meant.

"You need to come home," her mother said after a weighted pause. "You don't belong there."

"That's kind of the problem." Sienna swallowed against the emotion that threatened to choke her. "I don't belong anywhere."

She drove around for hours, up and down the streets of Crimson and out toward the mountain pass and the farms and ranches that surrounded the town. There was the turnoff for Crimson Ranch, a property she knew was owned by some famous actress. She'd read about it in a magazine a few years ago, and the casual mention of her hometown had been the thing to reawaken her curiosity about where she'd come from and the father and brother still there.

Even with that curiosity, she'd kept herself distant when Jase had come to visit their mother last year after Dana had finished her cancer treatments. Much like today, the reality of her past and her present colliding had been too much for Sienna.

She'd hidden out in her apartment for an entire weekend, as if she'd spontaneously stumble upon him at one of her favorite neighborhood haunts. Which was stupid because Chicago was enormous.

Unlike Crimson. She was tired and hungry and had squatted to go to the bathroom on the side of a deserted Forest Service road because she was too scared to even run into the local gas station and take the chance on an encounter with Jase.

She could return to The Bumblebee. Paige had told her she planned on painting one of the upstairs bedrooms

today. No doubt her new friend would be happy to see
her and to hear all about how the meeting with Declan
had gone.

Which was what kept Sienna from going back. How
could she admit that she'd run away after only a few
words with him? She hated that he'd surprised her instead
of the other way around. He'd known she was in town to
see him, and for some reason that seemed to take away
the power she'd expected to feel in the moment.

As she did another loop through downtown Crimson,
past painted Victorian houses that had been converted
into businesses and the tourists milling along the picturesque shop fronts, she spotted a white Jeep parked
at the curb, the words Crimson County Sheriff emblazoned on the side.

Her frustration coalesced into anger in an instant. She
should be able to approach her father and brother in her
own time, on her own terms. But that choice had been
taken away from her because they'd been warned about her.
Warned.

As if she were some criminal or loose cannon intent
on trouble.

Cole Bennett had called her a troublemaker, and obviously he believed it because he'd taken it upon himself to tell Jase she was in town. He'd stripped her of the
only power she had in this situation, and for that all of
her wrath narrowed with laser precision to focus on him.

She parked the rental car on a side street and stepped
out, surveying the block where Cole's Jeep was parked.
There was a florist on one side and a toy store next to
that. Several gift shops had wares displayed out on the
sidewalk, displays of home goods or racks of colorful
T-shirts.

About halfway down the block, she saw the sign for

Life is Sweet bakery and started walking. Cops and doughnuts might be a stereotype, but she figured a coffee shop was as good a place as any to start her search.

She pushed open the door, ignoring the way her stomach growled at the mouthwatering scent of yeasty dough and sugar that enveloped her.

A woman from behind the counter called out a greeting, but Sienna ignored her. She stalked toward the table at the far side, where a man sat, his caramel-colored hair tousled. His shoulders were so broad under his sheriff's uniform, they made him look almost out of place at one of the small café tables in the cheery space.

"You did this to me," she said, her voice trembling slightly.

Cole looked up like he didn't have a care in the world, arched a brow. "There are a lot of things I'd like to do to you, sweetheart. Care to elaborate on what you're talking about at the moment?"

Butterflies zipped through her stomach at the intensity in his gaze, and she hated him even more for being able to so casually defuse her righteous anger. Now she was distracted by him—his brown eyes studying her, the shadow of stubble that covered his jaw, his big hand holding tight to a thin ballpoint pen. He looked strong and sure, and Sienna craved that like she imagined her father still wanted a drink, despite his sobriety.

It made her feel weak and unsteady, one more reminder that the mask of confidence and poise she'd worn all these years was nothing but her pretending to be someone she wasn't.

"You told them I was coming." She lifted a hand, jabbed a finger at him. "You *warned* them."

He wrapped his giant hand around hers, folding her

fingers into her palm, then gently tugged her into the seat across from him.

She didn't fight because she was suddenly weary to the bone and grateful for the chair. The other customers had turned to stare, obviously curious about the crazy woman who'd go toe to toe with the hulking sheriff.

Cole pasted on a casual, good ol' boy type of smile, although his eyes told a different story. "Katie, would you mind sending over one of those amazing chicken salad sandwiches and a couple of lemonades?" He turned toward the counter. "Looks like I'm here for lunch after all."

"Sure thing, Sheriff," the pretty brunette at the cash register answered. "Chips or pasta salad on the side?"

Cole tossed a questioning gaze at Sienna. "Pasta salad," she mumbled after a moment and Cole put in the request.

"But I don't want anything," Sienna insisted, even though she could feel her hands trembling due to hunger. "I can handle myself just fine without your help."

"Marlene," Cole began conversationally. "She's my office manager and pretty much runs everything at the department. I might have mentioned her before?"

Sienna narrowed her eyes.

"Right." Cole sat back and studied her for a long moment. "Marlene is an undisputed genius and normally easy as pie to get along with. But if she gets too hungry… Well, she has a term for it. She calls it hangry." He inclined his head. "It's a mix of hungry and angr—"

"I know what hangry is," Sienna said, irritated that her snappish tone made her sound even hangrier than she was. "I had oatmeal for breakfast. I'm fine."

"What time did you eat breakfast?"

"Seven."

"That's five hours ago."

"A lawman and a mathematician. You really are all that and a bag of chips."

"Chips are good, but you made the right choice with pasta salad. It's homemade, along with the chicken salad. This place only recently started serving lunch. Katie Crawford, the owner, bakes all the bread herself. The fact that she's serving lunch has been kind of a game changer around here."

Cole Bennett was the biggest game changer Sienna had ever met. She'd come into the bakery to tell him off and somehow now they were having a casual conversation about food and hunger. She crossed her arms over her chest, unwilling to allow herself to be distracted any longer. She had business in Crimson, and she was done with the town's hottie sheriff inserting himself into it.

"I don't know—"

"Here's your sandwich. Hope you enjoy."

Sienna glanced up at the woman who'd approached the table, ready to snap out a scathing reprimand for being interrupted. One of the first things Craig Pierce had drilled into her was that good waitstaff should know their place. And interrupting a customer's conversation was tantamount to spitting in the food as far as her stepfather was concerned.

Sienna had never bought into the idea and had always been polite to everyone she met. Even though she'd been a "have" for over half her life, she never forgot what it felt like to be a "have not." But her temper was practically boiling over, and she didn't much care who bore the brunt of it.

Except all she could do when she turned to Katie Crawford was offer a small smile and a muttered "thank you."

Cole chuckled, as if he knew what she'd intended and was amused that she couldn't lash out at the bakery owner. But to unleash her temper on Katie would have been like kicking a week-old puppy. Maybe it was because she'd grown up in a big city, but Sienna didn't think she'd ever seen someone who oozed sweetness and inner goodness the way Katie did. It was a wonder she didn't have tiny bluebirds flitting around her head chirping a merry tune and anointing Katie with a crown of woven flowers.

"What's so funny about my chicken salad?" the woman asked Cole, hands on hips.

"Nothing at all," Cole said quickly. "Your food is always delicious and everyone in town knows it."

Katie beamed at Cole, then stuck out her hand toward Sienna. "Maybe not someone new to town. I'm Katie Crawford."

"Sienna Pierce."

"Nice to meet you, Sienna. What brings you to Crimson? How do you and Cole know each other? Can I bring you dessert for later?"

"That's a lot of questions," Sienna said, her stomach growling as she inhaled the delectable scent of tangy chicken salad and fresh bread.

Katie's smile widened even farther. "My husband says I'm too curious for my own good, but it's part of owning a business." She scrunched up her pert nose. "Plus we have a little one at home now, so work hours are about all the time I get to socialize."

"I saw the other ladies at monthly Mexican a couple of weeks ago," Cole said. "Noticed you weren't part of the group."

"Willow had a bad cold," Katie told him. "Noah was on an overnight doing trail maintenance on the other side of the pass, and I didn't want to get a sitter."

Sienna took a big bite of the sandwich, moaning softly

at the explosion of flavors that hit her tongue. She listened absently as Katie and Cole discussed Willow's cold and the various remedies Katie had tried to make her better.

"She's finally sleeping through the night again," Katie reported, then glanced toward Sienna. "Do you like it?"

"There aren't words," Sienna said around a mouthful, "for how much."

"I'll bring you a brownie for later. I don't think you ever mentioned what brought you to Crimson."

Sienna placed the uneaten portion of sandwich on the plate, then wiped her mouth with a napkin. "I'm visiting family."

"That's great." Katie clapped her hands together. "Anyone I know?"

Sienna shrugged and shot a look toward Cole.

"Katie is married to Emily's brother," he told her.

Her stomach pitched. "Of course she is." She closed her eyes for a moment, then forced herself to meet Katie's friendly gaze. "Jase is *my* brother."

She waited for Katie's expression to change, but if anything it gentled even more. "It's good to have you back in town. It can't be easy after all this time, but family is important no matter how much water has passed under the bridge."

Sienna opened her mouth to argue but found she couldn't. Although it was silly, the simple blessing from a relative stranger meant something to her.

"Isn't that right, Cole?" Katie asked quietly, and for the first time Sienna saw the unflappable sheriff look rattled.

"Sure, Katie. I'll have an iced tea if you don't mind?"

"Coming right up," Katie answered and turned away.

"You're hiding something," Sienna said, leaning forward across the table. "And Little Mrs. Sunshine knows what it is."

Cole made a dismissive sound low in his throat. "I'm not hiding anything." He snagged the remaining half a sandwich. "I also appreciate that you look less like you're going to claw my eyes out now that you've had something to eat. Want to tell me how that started?"

She picked up a fork and stabbed a piece of pasta. Her body was no longer bristling with anger now but the reminder of why she'd come in here in the first place made her chest ache.

"I saw Declan."

"It didn't go well?"

She took another bite of pasta salad, stared out the window of the bakery as she chewed, then turned back to Cole. "Before I could gather my courage to approach the door, he saw me. Went out the back door and slipped around my car to knock on the driver's side window." She blew out a breath. "Scared me half to death."

"Sounds like Declan. How did the conversation go?"

"Terrible. I freaked out. I wasn't ready. But he knew to expect me." She pointed a finger at Cole. "Because you warned Jase."

He closed his eyes for a moment, then said quietly, "I'm sorry, Sienna."

"Are you?"

"Jase is my friend," he told her as if that explained everything.

But the words only fueled her temper again. Jase was his friend. Katie was his friend. Crimson was his home. And Sienna was nothing.

It shouldn't surprise her or hurt her feelings, but it did. To the point that the pain and loneliness were like a tidal wave, crashing over and pulling her under. She couldn't breathe. She certainly wouldn't stay here and casually enjoy the food he'd ordered because he could read her better than anyone had done in ages.

Like that meant something. Like she meant something.

"Stay out of my business," she said, pushing back from the table. "My time in Crimson has nothing to do with you, Sheriff." She purposely used his title instead of his name, watching his eyes snap in response.

A tiny victory, but she'd take anything she could get at this point. She walked out of the bakery and away from Cole before she could change her mind.

Chapter Six

"It's bad in there."

Cole nodded as he tightened his flak vest. "You don't have to go in, Grant. Melody and the kids—"

His top deputy snorted. "Don't do that, boss. I knew the risks of this job when I took it, and so did Mel. You can't treat me like I'm a rookie."

Turning toward the darkened warehouse that sat on an abandoned property outside of town, Cole shook his head. "This is Crimson," he said, anger making his voice low. "We shouldn't have to be dealing with scumbags like this up here."

Grant shrugged. "The town is growing, and the world is changing. Big cities don't have the market cornered on lowlife drug dealers."

"It's a small operation." Cole inclined his head toward JJ Waring, a second deputy who stood about twenty feet from them, camouflaged by an overgrown bush and the darkness of the hour. "Waring and I can handle it."

"I'm fine, Sheriff." Grant moved so he was standing in front of Cole. "Elaina is fine."

Cole blew out a breath. Last fall, Grant's young daughter had gotten caught in the middle of an incident with a tweaked-out petty criminal who'd had too many run-ins with the department to count. But on that night, the man had gone too far, and Elaina had ended up hospitalized from a knife wound. Grant and his wife, Melody, had witnessed the whole thing.

Although everyone from Grant to Marlene to Jase had insisted it wasn't Cole's fault, he couldn't help but blame himself. There had been something about the man that had reminded Cole of his brother, Shep. The brother he hadn't seen in close to seven years. Cole had gone easy on the guy too many times, and his drug use and subsequent bad behavior had escalated.

Cole took his responsibilities as sheriff seriously, but his duty to the men and women who worked for him was even more important. He knew that each of them understood the risks involved but that didn't stop him from wanting to protect them, along with every person who lived under his jurisdiction.

Since that night last fall, he'd made it his personal mission to take down the underground drug ring that had spread its slimy tentacles up from Denver and into several of the high mountain communities.

It went beyond the legal marijuana that had become so popular in Colorado in the past few years. The stuff these guys were manufacturing was hard-core, and the bigger operations in the city had set up satellite sites in rural areas where there was more room and less monitoring by local law enforcement.

Not in Crimson if Cole had anything to do about it.

He unholstered his gun and nodded at Grant. "Glad to have you by my side," he said, and together they slipped into the shadows.

Sienna blinked awake, then glanced at the clock. Two in the morning.

She sighed and sat up, the sheets and comforter twisted into a ball at the foot of the bed. Maybe a glass of water would help—or warm milk. Anything to stop her from tossing and turning, sleep remaining elusive as her mind spun in a dozen different directions.

She went to the bedroom window, unlatched it, then pushed it open. Cool air was good for sleeping, too. Her gaze snagged on the familiar white Jeep parked at the curb in front of The Bumblebee. Was there something wrong in this quiet neighborhood to bring out Crimson's finest at this late hour?

The SUV was dark, no motor running. She couldn't see the driver but knew without a doubt that Cole was behind the wheel.

She hadn't seen him since yesterday at the bakery, and tried to ignore the thrill that zipped along her skin at the mere thought of him now.

After walking away from him, she'd planned to march down the street to the mayor's office in the county courthouse, a redbrick historic building situated across the park that made up the center of downtown Crimson.

But the thought of facing her brother made her break out in a cold sweat, heart pounding and hands trembling. Why was it so difficult to face Jase or her father?

Her mother had been the one to take her away from Crimson, but Sienna still felt the painful sting of rejection from being let go so easily. The argument could be made that her life had been better far away from the turmoil of her alcoholic father—she knew her mother would contend that Sienna had been given many more opportunities in Chicago than she ever would have had in Crimson.

That didn't matter either. She'd felt expendable. Even though they'd both been kids, Jase had stayed in Crimson because Declan had needed him, not Sienna. The two Crenshaw men were a pair, and she was an outsider in the town where she'd been born.

Not allowing herself to think too much about her actions, she padded downstairs, slipped on a pair of shoes and let herself out the front door. The driver's side window lowered as she rounded the front of the Jeep.

"Is there a problem, Sheriff?" She wrapped her arms around her waist, still surprised by the nip in the air. The temperature in the mountains dipped every night when the sun went down, so different from the Midwest, where it often stayed within a few degrees of the sweltering heat and humidity of daylight hours.

"No." The one syllable was a low rumble. Cole's face remained in shadow, but something was different tonight. The invisible current that seemed to connect them was still there, but there was an unusual charge to it.

"Was my restless sleep disturbing the neighbors tonight?"

"I didn't get a call from the neighbors."

She stepped closer to the SUV. "Then why are you—" She sucked in a breath. "What happened? You're hurt."

He was leaning back against the headrest and shifted to meet her gaze fully. "I'm fine. Just not ready to go home."

"The bandage on your shoulder doesn't look fine," she insisted, reaching for the door. "Oh, my God, Cole. Were you shot?"

He didn't argue when she reached around him to unfasten the seat belt. He wore a white T-shirt with one sleeve bunched above the bandage that covered the upper part of his arm. "You said my name again." One side of his mouth curved. "It sounds good coming from your lips."

"You're delirious. We need to get you to the hospital."

"I'm fine. Bullet grazed me."

"Who shot you?" she demanded, tugging him from the Jeep.

"Bad guy," he muttered.

"There's a cut on your forehead."

"It's only a scratch. I chased him through the woods."

She took his hand and led him up the flagstone walkway toward the house. Paige was a deep sleeper, so Sienna didn't think the inn owner would wake up, but she climbed the stairs to her bedroom quietly, Cole following behind her.

She pushed him toward the bed. "Sit down," she ordered. "I'm going to get something to clean out that cut."

"Scratch," he insisted.

"Tomato, to-mah-to," she shot back and hurried toward the bathroom at the end of the hall. She found a bottle of hydrogen peroxide, cotton balls and a small box of bandages, returning to the bedroom to find Cole sprawled across the bed.

He glanced at her as she moved toward him. "Nice wallpaper," he said, circling a finger in the air.

A rose-hued paper with a pattern of red and pink roses covered the walls. The queen-size bed had a wrought-iron frame in a delicate design with filigree decorating the end of each post. There was a tall chest of drawers against one wall, and a shorter, longer dresser on the opposite wall. Both were covered with lace doilies and vases of dried flowers.

It was like a throwback to an inn of a hundred years ago, and Sienna had immediately appreciated all the homey touches. It was a feminine space, but even on his back, Cole looked ridiculously masculine in it.

"Tell me what happened." She sat on the edge of the bed, placing the supplies on the nightstand.

"Drug bust," he said tightly. "More guys than we anticipated."

"A drug bust in Crimson?" She soaked a cotton ball with hydrogen peroxide. "That seems hard to believe."

"I only wish our mountain Mayberry, as you call it, was safe from the issues people associate with big cities. But drugs are an insidious problem. Maybe not to the level other places find, but we deal with our share of bad here, Sienna."

"Was it a success?"

He nodded, then hissed out a breath when she dabbed the cotton ball against his broken skin. "Did you ever consider a career as a nurse?"

She smiled sweetly and pressed harder against the cut. "I should take you to the hospital."

He gave a small laugh. "Spent some time there earlier and not going back. One of my deputies shot a guy who was fleeing the scene. He'll live, but his leg needed some attention." He moved his arm, then groaned. "The doc wrapped up my shoulder so I know it's fine."

"Was anyone…?"

"Killed? No, thankfully. But we arrested four of them and shut down the local operation. It was a good night."

She took a bandage strip from the box and unpeeled the wrapper. "So why are you here?"

"I really am sorry," he said quietly. "Not that I told Jase about you being in town, but that he and Declan knowing seems to be messing with your head."

"My head is fine," she whispered, covering his cut with the bandage.

"Your head is gorgeous," he countered, "just like the rest of you. I didn't intend to hurt you, Sienna."

"The road to hell…" she said, making her voice light. Pretending it didn't mean anything to her that he'd come here tonight.

Not fooling either of them.

He encircled her wrist with his big hand. "I'm sorry."

She nodded, ignoring the butterflies fluttering through her chest. "I probably would have freaked out either way. Somehow the idea of facing Jase and my dad is way different than the reality of it."

"But you're still here."

"Call me a glutton for punishment, but I'm not ready to give up quite yet."

"Good."

She tugged out of his grasp, stood and walked to the window. "You're in my bed," she told him, stating the obvious.

He flashed a wry smile, sat up and placed his feet on the floor. "I should go."

"You can stay," she blurted, feeling color flood her cheeks as he arched a brow.

"Sienna."

"I don't mean I'm going to sleep with you." She pressed her fingers to her flaming cheeks. "Or I guess I do mean sleep. But nothing else. No hanky-panky."

"Hanky-panky," Cole murmured.

She rolled her eyes, walking to the opposite side of the bed. "I remember my…Declan using that term when Jase and I were little, before Mom and I left, of course. There was a young couple that moved into the trailer next to ours for just a few months, but they were quite enamored of each other. When Jase asked why they turned off the lights and went to bed so early every night, Declan answered 'hanky-panky.'" She reached down and smoothed a hand over the pillowcase. "I didn't even understand what he meant, but the phrase stuck with me."

"It's strange the things we remember from childhood."

"Tell me something funny from when you were a kid," she said, slipping between the cool sheets and leaning back against the headboard.

Whether from her proximity or the thought of having to share something personal, she saw Cole's shoulders stiffen. Maybe he'd shut her out, as he had the other night. But she wouldn't regret her curiosity. He was like a puzzle she couldn't stop trying to solve.

He straightened from the bed, massaged the back of his neck with one hand. "We moved every couple of years because of my dad's career in the army. Me and my twin brother, Shep—"

"You have a twin brother?" she asked, stunned. "I thought you said your family was gone."

His jaw clenched. "They are. My parents are dead, and Shep could be for all I know. We haven't spoken in years, and he seemed hell-bent on destruction before he left. I don't even know where he is at this point."

"But you could—"

"Do you want the funny story or not?"

She clamped her mouth shut and nodded.

"Shep and I are identical, so we did a lot of pretending we were each other, especially when we first got to a new school. Fourth grade in Germany, we spent an entire semester taking tests for each other because we were in different classes. They wanted to suspend both of us but couldn't prove anything."

Sienna gave a small laugh. "Was your mom mad?"

"She dragged us down to a local barber and flipped a coin to decide which one of us had to have our head shaved." As he spoke, he toed off first one boot, then the other. Sienna's heart raced in response. "From that day on, we weren't allowed to have the same haircut because she never wanted us to be able to play that kind of trick again."

"I bet you found other ways to be bad."

"Plenty of them."

"I was a good girl," she blurted as he moved toward the door and flipped off the lights, plunging the room into darkness.

"I never had a doubt," he told her, and she could hear the humor in his voice, "despite the speeding and the car-borrowing and all the other trouble I'm sure you're going to cause while you're in town."

She pulled the covers tighter around her. "I meant what I said, Cole."

"God, it kills me when you say my name." The mattress dipped as he lowered himself to the bed again.

"Should I stick to 'Sheriff'?"

"You know the answer to that, and I know the no hanky-panky rule." He shifted, stretching out on his back. "But I'm tired as hell after the night I had, Sienna, so I'm going to take you up on the offer of sleeping together." He smiled. "Emphasis on sleeping."

"You're laying on top of the covers," she pointed out.

"Safer this way, sweetheart." She heard him yawn and turned on her side. It was a crazy offer she'd made and even crazier that he'd taken her up on it, but there was something comforting about Cole's big body next to her on the bed. She felt less alone, safer—although she had no reason not to feel safe. But she'd been off-kilter since the moment she'd arrived in Colorado.

Now she took a deep breath and closed her eyes, her weary body practically melting into the soft mattress.

"Good night, Cole," she whispered.

"Good night, Sienna. Sweet dreams."

Chapter Seven

Cole winced as the second stair from the bottom squeaked under his foot. It was five in the morning, and he was working on three hours of sleep—albeit the best sleep he'd had in years. He'd drifted off almost as soon as he closed his eyes, then woken a few minutes ago with Sienna snuggled tight against his chest, his arm wrapped around her waist.

He'd wanted to run his hands along her curves, to kiss the sweet spot at the base of her neck, to press himself into her—all those things and more. But she'd said no "hanky-panky" and he was going to honor that request, even if it killed him. So he'd gingerly climbed out of bed, grabbed his boots and let himself out of her bedroom without waking her.

He sure as hell didn't need any early morning runners to notice his patrol Jeep in front of The Bumblebee and start asking questions. Crimson was a small town and a close-knit community and gossip traveled faster than a prairie fire across the drought-plagued plains.

"Coffee, Sheriff?"

He cursed under his breath, then pasted on a smile as he turned to meet Paige's questioning gaze. "I'll get some at the station later."

"You must have arrived late last night," she said conversationally, sipping from a mug that said *I drink coffee for your protection*. "Now you're heading out before sunrise."

"This is not what it looks like," he said through clenched teeth.

"Is that so?" She scrunched up her nose. "Because despite the fact that you seem a little worse for wear with those bandages, it looks like a booty call."

"Nothing happened between Sienna and me." He ran a hand through his hair, unable to figure out how to explain why he'd parked in front of the inn last night in the first place. Not when he barely understood the reasons himself. "I was here but we slept. Not together. Next to each other. That's all."

She studied him for a moment, then nodded. "Okay."

"Okay? Just like that?"

"I don't know you well, Sheriff, but you don't strike me as a liar. Plus, I think you like Sienna." She wiggled her eyebrows. "You really like her."

He didn't bother to deny it. "It doesn't matter how I feel about her. She's here temporarily. She could leave town at any time."

"Even she isn't sure how long she'll stay," Paige agreed. "I guess it depends on how things go with Jase and her dad, whenever she actually has a real conversation with either of them." She shook her head. "Family stuff is always more complicated than you want it to be."

Cole thought of his parents and his brother, of the lies and drama that tore apart his family. His biggest regret in life was being unable to fix what his father broke.

"Yeah. Would you mind not mentioning me being here to anyone? I don't want…"

"You like her," Paige told him. "That matters. She needs someone in her corner."

Cole blew out a breath. How could he be in Sienna's corner and still remain loyal to his friendship with Jase? But he couldn't deny the connection he felt to her.

"I've got to go. Thanks for understanding."

She smiled. "I don't understand it, but I don't need to. Just don't hurt her and we'll have no problems."

"I'll do my best," he promised with a low chuckle, then let himself out the front door. It was funny to think of the petite inn owner, with her bohemian dresses and crazy curly hair, giving him an implied threat. He couldn't imagine what kind of problem Paige could possibly create for someone like him, but he still appreciated her loyalty.

He glanced at Sienna's bedroom window as he climbed into the Jeep and turned the key in the ignition, his shoulder still aching. Where did last night leave the two of them? As he drove through town toward his house on the other side of Crimson Creek, those late-night hours spent in Sienna's bed felt more and more like a dream.

He showered, grabbed a stale bagel from the cabinet, then headed to the station. He checked in with a couple of his deputies, then called the county jail to get an update on the men they'd arrested. There was a mountain of paperwork to process, and he was on his fourth cup of coffee when a knock sounded on the door to his office.

"You got a minute?" Jase asked, peering in. "I brought muffins from Life is Sweet if that makes a difference."

"Katie's muffins make all the difference." Cole sat

back, stretched his arms over his head and then winced at the pain in his arm. "Come on in and have a seat."

"I heard last night was intense."

"Yeah."

"But you took down Elton's operation." Jase set the brown bag from the bakery on Cole's desk, then folded his tall body into a chair.

Cole inclined his head. "For now. The guys running the bigger operation in Denver will have another lackey in place within months. We need to make sure we don't let down our guard."

"It was still a win," Jase insisted. "Can you ever just take credit for something and bask in the glory for a day?"

"There's no glory in what we did last night. But I'm grateful my men came out unscathed."

"What about your shoulder and face?"

"Minor."

"Of course."

Cole reached in the bag and pulled out a blueberry muffin, his favorite. "Did you come here for an official report on last night?" He took a big bite, tossing the remainder of his bagel in the trash as he did.

Jase gripped the arms of the chair, his shoulders stiffening. "She saw my dad."

"Her dad, too," Cole said quietly, choosing not to mention he knew all about Sienna's encounter with Declan. It would reveal too much when he wasn't sure yet what Jase wanted from him.

"Apparently she sat in her car in front of his duplex."

"No law against that."

Jase blew out a breath. "Dad noticed and walked out to talk to her. But she took off right after. Now he's worked up that he scared her away and wants me to reach out."

"Okay."

"Not okay," Jase countered. "I don't know what to say to her. I have no idea what she wants or why she's still in town when she hasn't talked to either of us."

"Maybe she's getting her bearings," Cole suggested.

"What does that mean?"

"We both know she didn't plan this trip. She might need some time to figure out exactly what she wants from a relationship with you and Declan."

"I don't believe she wants any kind of relationship." Jase shook his head. "I think she's hanging around to stir the pot. I get the feeling she's angry with both of us, although I can't figure out why. Hell, she was the one who got out. I stayed behind and dealt with Dad's demons while Sienna lived the good life in Chicago."

Cole concentrated on pulling the wrapper from the oversize muffin. He took another bite, then a long drink of coffee. He'd hoped Jase would just continue his rant, but obviously he wanted Cole's take on the situation.

"You chose to stay."

"It wasn't much of a choice," Jase muttered.

"But you got to make it. Maybe the life you had was difficult, but it was yours. Your mom took Sienna. She had no choice."

"Are you telling me I got the better deal spending my childhood trying to keep Declan away from the bottle—unsuccessfully for years as everyone knows? I went to my mom's house last year when I was in Chicago. Remember the movie *Home Alone*?"

Cole nodded.

"They live around the corner from the house where it was filmed. It's a hell of a nice neighborhood. That's where Sienna grew up. She went to great schools, played tennis and rode horses if the framed photos our mom has displayed are any indication. Am I supposed to feel sorry for her?"

"You know a bunch of material crap doesn't necessarily make for a happy childhood."

"You're defending her."

"There's nothing to defend, Jase." Cole blew out a breath. "I'm telling you that from what I gather, the grass wasn't always green for Sienna, despite where she was raised."

"I need her gone," Jase said suddenly.

"Why?"

"It's not the right time. We're about to have a baby. Em is worried about how Davey is going to take to having a little sister or brother. He seems excited by it now, but it's going to be a lot of work."

Cole knew that Emily's son from her first marriage had Asperger's syndrome, and helping him manage social situations and interactions with other people had been Emily's priority for years.

"Work is crazy busy," Jase went on. "Did you hear a private equity group out of California bought the old ski resort?"

"Seriously?"

Jase nodded. "Colorado has had some great ski seasons the past few years, but the popular places are getting too crowded. There aren't too many independently owned mountains left, but if these people get the resort and the lifts operational again, it would be a game changer for the town."

"That's great, I guess," Cole said, although he thought Crimson was just fine the way it was. "But none of what you've told me has anything to do with Sienna."

"It's not her exactly," Jase said with a sigh. "It's everything—the baby, working with the resort's new owner, plus my dad. Mainly my dad. He's been doing great since we moved him into his new house. But the last time he fell off the wagon, it was after he got the letter from Mom. Now Sienna shows up here and he's worked up about it." He rubbed a hand across his jaw. "I know his issues aren't her fault, but the timing of her coming back into his life…"

"Why are you telling me all this?"

"You know her."

"She's been in town less than a week."

Jase lifted a brow. "Katie told Emily you bought her lunch the other day."

"People around here talk to each other entirely too much."

"True," Jase agreed. "But maybe you can help with Sienna. I don't want to set her off—"

"You're not at all interested in having a relationship with her?"

"I'm not against it. But I'm not sure I trust her motivation. My mom reached out to me last year, and I saw her in Chicago. She was going through cancer treatments and her desire to reconnect with me seemed genuine. Then she let it slip that her husband was brokering some big merger at work and couldn't have any whiff of scandal attached to his name."

"How are you a scandal?"

"It was during the mayoral election, and the other company was headquartered in Denver. I'm not sure what was going into the deal or why her background mattered to anyone. But it was like she was trying to acknowledge she had a past in Colorado while still making sure it didn't affect her current life."

"That's cold."

"Don't get me wrong, we had a fine visit. She genuinely feels guilty about ripping apart our family the way she did. I also think she'd do anything to protect the life she has now. Maybe it was more like she was putting her affairs in order, although now that she's in remission I haven't heard from her. Bottom line is it all felt too coincidental in timing, like there was an underlying agenda I wasn't privy to."

Jase shrugged. "I don't know Sienna, but it makes sense that she'd be cut from the same cloth. Will you talk to her?"

Cole wanted to agree to help. He didn't have family in his life, and his friends meant all the more to him because of it. But he couldn't make his mouth form the words. Not after spending the wee hours last night with Sienna tucked against his body, even with the bedclothes separating them.

"I can't get involved like that."

Jase stared at him for a long moment, then closed his eyes and let out a soft laugh. "She's more like my mother than I even realized."

"What does that mean?"

"I heard a ton of stories growing up about my dad's side of the family. The Crenshaws are infamous around Crimson as a bunch of hard-drinking, hard-living hooligans. It took a lot of work to make people in this town believe I wasn't like that."

"You do look remarkably like your great-great grandfather."

Among a group of pictures that displayed life in the early days of Crimson was a sepia-colored photo in the county courthouse of a man sitting in the original town jail. A man who happened to be Jase's forefather. Cole had been shocked when he'd first met Jase at his resemblance to "Black Jack" Crenshaw.

"Trust me, I know." Jase blew out a breath. "But I also heard plenty of stories about my mother—how pretty she was, how she could have had any man in town when she arrived here with her family from Alabama. People couldn't seem to stop speculating on why she'd chosen my father. Of course, no one was surprised when their marriage fell apart. But Sienna must take after her in some ways if she already has you wrapped around her finger."

Cole bristled at the implied accusation. "I'm not wrapped around her finger," he shot back, "but I get what it's like to be alone."

"She's not alone," Jase countered.

"She is," Cole insisted. "And whatever her reasons are for coming here, she's not looking to cause trouble for you." It was funny he could assure Jase with no reservations, even though Sienna was the most troubling thing that had hit his life in years.

"I hope not." Jase ran a hand through his hair and stood. "At least keep an eye on her. That shouldn't be too difficult."

"Give her a chance, Jase."

"Maybe I will," his friend agreed as he backed toward the door. "I just hope you don't give her too big of one."

Chapter Eight

Later that morning, Sienna walked into Life is Sweet, her stomach in knots. Pretending like she belonged in Crimson seemed to be almost as difficult as gathering the courage to talk to her father or brother.

But she couldn't spend her day holed up at the inn, especially with Paige dropping not-so-subtle hints about Cole. Sienna still wasn't sure what she'd been thinking inviting him into the house—and into her bed. All she knew was she'd slept better in those hours she was next to him than she had in ages.

Paige wasn't much for subtlety, so as soon as Sienna had walked down the stairs, the innkeeper handed her a cup of coffee and a box of condoms.

"Here at The Bumblebee," she'd said with a smile, "we like to make sure our guests haven't forgotten anything they might need during their stay."

"It wasn't like that," Sienna had insisted.

"Then you're not as smart as you look. That man is gorgeous and I'll tell you if a hot guy ended up in my bed—no matter the reason—I wouldn't squander my opportunity."

Sienna wasn't sure what kind of opportunity she wanted with the town's sexy sheriff, but she knew she wasn't ready to talk about it. She'd taken the condoms and the coffee and returned to her room with the excuse of having to call her office in Chicago.

That part wasn't a lie. Before she left for Aspen, she'd been working on a big ad campaign for a multinational telecommunication company ready to roll out its latest device. Although her extended stay in Colorado complicated things, she could do most of the work remotely.

She'd sent out a round of emails to her team, then tweaked a presentation her assistant had sent her the night before. Her boss was being patient because he needed Sienna's reputation and the relationships she'd cultivated with their client base, but she knew that wouldn't last forever.

The hotel in Aspen had delivered her luggage, and while her clothes weren't perfect for Crimson's casual vibe, at least they were hers. Now she had to come up with a plan for her time in Crimson and figure out how long she was planning to stay. For that, she needed more coffee and one of the muffins she'd seen in the glass display counter of the bakery.

Katie, the bakery's owner, was nowhere in sight as Sienna approached the counter, and a strange sense of disappointment washed over her. The woman had been friendly, even after Cole explained who she was. Sienna secretly looked forward to another conversation with someone who didn't seem either fascinated by or skeptical of her past in Crimson.

She ordered a coffee and muffin, then turned to find a beautiful and very pregnant woman staring at her.

"Even if I hadn't Googled you, I'd know who you are," the woman told her, one hand coming to rest on her belly in an oddly protective gesture. "You and Jase must have looked like twins as kids."

"I don't have photos," Sienna answered automatically, then took her drink as the barista placed it on the counter. She didn't need to ask the woman's identity. This had to be Emily, her brother's wife. Sienna's sister-in-law. The thought of it was both strange and oddly appealing.

At least it would have been in a perfect world. But not with how Emily was glaring at her. This was one confrontation Sienna knew she wouldn't be able to get out of so easily.

"Your dad does." Emily's eyes narrowed. "In fact, a framed photo of you has pride of place on the mantel in his new house. Maybe you would have found that out if you hadn't run off like a big chicken when he spoke to you."

Sienna heard the sharp intake of breath from the woman behind the counter. She turned and took the bag with the muffin the woman handed her, offering a smile and ignoring the fact that her fingers trembled. *Big chicken.* Good to know Emily Crenshaw didn't hold back.

Sienna had spent a lifetime tiptoeing around difficult conversations. Her mother preferred the don't ask/don't tell school of thought for any topic thornier than which strand of pearls to wear to the country club for her weekly ladies' luncheon.

So the issues and questions Sienna had throughout her childhood consumed her body from the inside out.

And with that one snappish comment, Emily set lighter fluid to the flame and Sienna's entire being was engulfed. The mask she'd worn for years burned to ash, leaving her true self standing raw and new. Somehow it was a liberating sensation.

She straightened her shoulders and inclined her head. "I was seven when my mother put me in that car and drove away. For years, I waited for a letter or phone call from my dad. Every birthday, each Christmas. I wanted him to care that I was gone. I wanted him to find me. But he never did. He never even tried."

"You don't know what—"

Sienna held up a hand. "He had Jase because Jase was the one he needed. So if you think I'm going to go all misty-eyed and sentimental over the fact that he still has a left-behind picture of me on display, think again."

Suddenly she understood why she couldn't force herself to confront her father or brother. The pain might pour out, and then they'd see—everyone would see—how much it hurt her to be taken away from her life in this town.

Even though her childhood had been far from perfect, she'd belonged, unlike the way she'd been raised in Chicago, where she was constantly reminded of how grateful she should be for the advantages her mother's marriage to Craig Pierce had given both of them.

But to Sienna, those advantages had felt like a straitjacket. Having Emily try to confront her was like breaking free, and the tumble of emotions was overwhelming and devastating. She no longer cared who heard their conversation.

Sienna was done hiding her crazy.

"How about the years in between and the memories that could have—should have—been captured? Maybe

I'm more interested in the things in my life he missed."
She leaned in slightly. "But I'm sure not interested in
being lectured on how I handle myself now. So back off,
sister-in-law."

Emily's blue eyes widened slightly, but she didn't back
down. "I won't let you hurt my family."

"Is that why you think I'm here?"

"If you're anything like your mother," Emily said,
arching an eyebrow, "then yes."

"I'm nothing like her," Sienna said, but she couldn't be
sure that was true. Dana had tried her best to mold Sienna
into her own image. Sienna had followed along because
she hadn't felt like there was another choice. How much
of it had become embedded into the fiber of who she was
remained to be seen away from her mother's influence.

Her comment seemed to surprise Emily, and she nodded
slightly. "We'll see about that. Come to dinner tonight."

Sienna felt her mouth drop open. "You just read me
the riot act about not messing with you, and now you're
inviting me to dinner? Are you nuts?"

"Rhetorical question," a voice chimed in and both
women turned to see Katie standing behind the cash
registers. "Don't question how Emily's mind works. It's
a mystery to us all."

"Very funny," Emily muttered, but Sienna felt an
easing in the tension rolling off her brother's wife. She
expected nothing less from the sweet-tempered bakery
owner. Katie Crawford could likely tame a grizzly bear
by whispering lullabies into its furry ear.

"Not as funny as most of my customers watching this
little exchange with great fascination." Katie inclined
her head. "I'm pretty sure Mrs. Wasinski recorded the
whole thing on her new smartphone. If we're lucky,

she'll upload the video to Facebook and tag you both." Saccharine-sweet sarcasm dripped from her tone.

Emily whipped around and pointed at an elderly woman in a lavender tracksuit and thick hiking boots. "Delete it, Mrs. W., or I'm going to take Ruby for an after-dinner walk every night this month and let her poop in your rosebushes."

"You wouldn't dare," the woman said, looking shocked. "My roses took first place in the county fair last year."

"Then you probably don't want extra fertilizer on them."

"I assume Ruby is your dog," Sienna said, "and not your daughter."

"Best dog ever," Emily confirmed. She patted her belly. "My girl is on the way."

Mrs. Wasinski messed with her phone for several seconds before looking up again. "I don't care what Jase has done for this town, the Crenshaws have always been trouble, whether they grew up in Crimson or married into the family."

"Thanks for your opinion," Emily said sweetly as the older woman hurried out of the bakery.

"You're chasing off my customers now," Katie said with a groan.

Emily rolled her eyes. "She'll be back. No one can stay away from here for long." She turned her full attention on Sienna again. "Dinner at six tonight."

"I don't think—"

"You don't have to think. Just show up. If you're not here to make trouble, that's fine. If you are, we need to deal with it sooner than later because when this baby comes I need Jase's full attention."

Sienna glanced at Katie, who shrugged. "She won't take no for an answer at this point."

"Will you and your husband be there?" Sienna asked Katie.

"You need a buffer between yourself and your family?" Emily demanded.

Sienna winced slightly but nodded. "It can't hurt."

"Noah and Katie will be there then. I'll call my brother and tell him the good news," Emily said. "He's got dinner plans."

"I'll bring dessert," Katie offered.

"Make it chocolate," Emily said, then added, "Please." She pulled a small notepad from her purse, scribbled something on it and handed a sheet of paper to Sienna. "Here's our address. See you tonight."

"Um...thanks."

With a sharp nod, Emily turned and walked out of the bakery. Sienna let out a long breath as she stared at the address written on the slip of paper. Family dinner.

"Here you go." She looked up to find that Katie had walked around to the front of the counter. She handed Sienna another brown paper bag. "It's banana nut to go with your blueberry. I figure after that it could be a two-muffin morning."

"Thanks." Sienna took the bag. "Is she always so intense?"

"More so with the pregnancy. She really loves your brother."

"My brother," Sienna repeated softly. "Family dinner at my brother's house."

"Ready or not," Katie told her, as if reading Sienna's mind.

"Ready or not," Sienna agreed.

* * *

"I'm coming," Cole called, muting the baseball game he'd been watching and straightening from the couch. "No need to break down the door."

The pounding at his front door stopped as he approached it. Through the gauzy curtains he hadn't bothered to change when he bought the house last year, he saw the outline of a slender woman, her blond hair pulled back in a low ponytail.

"How did you find out where I live?" he asked as he opened the door.

Sienna stood on the front porch, her arms wrapped tightly around her waist. "Is it a secret? Do you call it the Sheriffcave?"

"Not quite," he said, trying to get his bearings. He still felt off-kilter from spending the night with her, and having her so close made him remember all the things about the previous night he'd been trying to force himself to forget. The warmth of her body, the scent of her hair as it tickled his cheek, how soft her skin was at the crook of her neck.

"Are you going to invite me in then?" One delicate brow lifted. "Because that would be the polite thing to do."

"Yeah, I'm real concerned about good manners," he said with a laugh but stepped back so she could walk past him into the house. She wore a pale pink scoop neck cotton shirt and slim jeans that grazed her ankles. As he'd come to expect, her makeup was minimal, and he had the urge to trace his finger along her cheek to feel its softness. She didn't yet look at home in Colorado but seemed less buttoned-up than she had that first day she'd arrived in town. As if the casual vibe of Crimson was slowly rubbing off on her.

An emotion he didn't recognize flared low in his belly as he watched her examine the space. He'd never brought a woman to his house. Hell, his dating life had been almost nonexistent since he'd moved to Crimson. Cole was dedicated to his job, and up until the past few days, that had been enough.

"Did you just move in?" she asked, her gaze snagging on a stack of cardboard boxes pushed against one wall.

"About a year ago," he admitted. "I've been too busy to deal with unpacking everything."

She inclined her head toward the muted television and the half-empty beer bottle and bag of chips on the coffee table. "Clearly."

"What's going on?" he asked. "Or did you stop by for the sole purpose of critiquing my interior decorating skills?"

"I need you to go to dinner with me," she blurted.

"Okay," he said slowly. "Did you have someplace special in mind?"

"I met my sister-in-law today," she continued. "She invited me to dinner. I'm supposed to be there in…" She glanced at the chunky silver watch that encircled her wrist. "Ten minutes."

"Emily invited you for dinner?" Cole tried to hide his shock, especially after Jase had told him he didn't trust Sienna. "And you want me to go with you?"

"Katie and her husband will be there, too." She walked forward and ran a hand along the back of his leather couch. "But they're Team Jase. I need someone on my side."

"You think that's me?" Pride and disbelief warred inside him at the idea that he was the one she'd come to for support. He realized she knew very few people in town, but still—

"You're all I've got," she muttered, then made a face. "Sorry. I didn't mean it to come out that way."

"You know Jase is my best friend," he said. "I'm the one who told him you'd come to town. You might remember raking me over the coals in the bakery."

"So all of this is really your fault." She flashed a smile that was more like a baring of teeth from a grizzly bear facing off with a mountain lion. "You have to go."

"What if I have plans?"

She glanced at the television, then back at him. "Are they important?"

"Give me a minute to change clothes."

"Thank you," she said softly, her gaze dropping to the ground as if she couldn't bear to make eye contact. He wondered what he'd see in her beautiful blue gaze right now. Unable to resist, he moved toward her and placed a finger under her chin, tipping it up until she looked at him.

It was all there—pain, loneliness, vulnerability and the smallest sliver of hope. As much as she pretended otherwise, Sienna wanted things to work out with Jase and her father. This night meant something to her. More than she probably knew.

Cole felt the heavy weight of responsibility settle on his shoulders, but to his surprise, he didn't immediately want to shrug it off. He had no problem with work responsibility but kept his personal life clean and simple because it was easier that way—no chance for mess or for anyone to get hurt. But he couldn't seem to keep Sienna at arm's length, and the more time he spent with her, the more he wanted to pull her in closer.

"It's going to be fine," he told her and brushed his lips across hers.

"Only if we're not late," she said, her breath tickling his skin.

He drew back, dropped a quick kiss on her nose and headed toward his bedroom.

Chapter Nine

"We should have sex."

Sienna threw a sidelong glance at Cole. Her stomach flipped up and down after she made the suggestion, like she was being pummeled by a tropical storm.

He stopped dead in his tracks, staring at the cobblestone walkway before them, and massaged a hand over the back of his neck. "Uh...do you have any context you want to offer with that suggestion?"

They were standing at the edge of sidewalk in front of Jase and Emily's house. Sienna was about to spend an evening with her father and brother for the first time in twenty years. The thought made her terrified, and fear made her say stupid things.

"You want to, right?" she demanded, turning to face Cole.

He looked down, desire and amusement both clear in his gaze. "Yes, but I don't think that's the point at the moment."

"No one has seen us yet. We could turn right around and drive back to your house." She held up her hands like she was showing off the grand prize in a game show contest. As if she were the prize, when they both knew she was anything but at the moment.

The words coming out of her mouth sounded crazy to her own ears, but she couldn't stop them. "Or we could get a hotel room. Not The Bumblebee. That would be weird with Paige there. Does Crimson have any rent-by-the-hour motels?"

He shook his head. "Not as far as I know."

"Your place then." She grabbed his hand and turned for the truck he drove when he wasn't on duty.

Cole didn't budge, and trying to get him to move was like tugging on a mountain.

"Sienna."

"Is it yes or no?" She tried to pull her hand away from his when it was clear he wasn't moving, but he held tight. "Because I could find someone else."

She gave a little yelp as she was suddenly plastered against the hard front of Cole's body. "No one else," he said, his voice a gravelly purr. "But right now we're having dinner at Jase's house. A dinner you invited me to about eight minutes ago. We couldn't be late and all that."

"Changed my mind."

"No."

"Yes," she insisted, letting her tone become peevish. "It's my mind and I get to do with it what I want. Along with my body."

"Duly noted," he said, infinitely patient. "I told you, tonight is going to be fine."

She bit down on her lip when a whimper threatened to escape. She swallowed and shook her head. "It's not going to be fine. I shouldn't be here. I should never have come in the first place. If they'd wanted to see me, they would have. It's been two decades and—"

"Jase said he came to Chicago last year. You didn't see him."

She spread her fingers out along his chest, letting the heat of his body seep into her palms. Wanting to curl against him but forcing herself to take a step back in case anyone inside the house was looking. "He was there because my mom summoned him. No one refuses Dana Pierce."

She sighed when Cole grimaced.

"I know I sound harsh," she told him. "But that's how my mom is about things. She's in remission now, and I'm grateful but I couldn't be a part of it at that time. And now..."

"Now is your chance."

"These aren't my people," she said, feeling miserable and alone.

"I'm your person."

"You're Jase's friend," she countered, refusing to allow herself to hold on to his words the way her heart wanted to. "You said so yourself."

"Tonight I'm yours." He laced his fingers with hers and started forward. "I've got your back."

She allowed him to lead her, knowing she wouldn't be able to make her legs move if he wasn't next to her.

"You ring the bell," he told her when they were on the porch.

She knocked instead, earning a smile from Cole. "A rebel at heart," he murmured. "You'll fit in just fine, sweetheart."

The door opened to reveal Jase Crenshaw standing on the other side. He was taller than Cole, probably close to six foot four, lanky and handsome and familiar to Sienna even as much as he was a stranger.

"I wasn't expecting to see you tonight," he said to Cole, looking more confused than surprised. "How many times have you been invited over but always managed not to make it?"

Cole flinched but covered it with a small laugh. "I made it tonight."

"I invited him," Sienna offered.

Jase raised a brow. "I'm glad you *both* could make it."

"Your wife didn't seem like she was going to take no for an answer."

"That's Emily," he agreed, smiling.

Sienna glanced over her shoulder toward Cole's truck. "I brought a bottle of wine but left it in the truck. I'll go—"

"I'll get it," Cole offered and jogged down the walkway toward the street before she could argue.

"Is wine okay?" she asked, turning back to Jase. "I forgot about your dad being sober and—"

"It's fine. And he's your dad, too," Jase added quietly. "He's doing well right now, but sobriety and Declan are fickle companions."

"I'm not going to do anything to sabotage him." Sienna clasped her hands in front of her stomach. "I just want you to know I'm not here to cause trouble for either of you."

"I'd ask why you are here," Jase said, stepping back into the house and gesturing for her to follow, "but I suppose you'll let us know that in your own time."

"Do you remember me?" she asked suddenly. "From when we were kids."

Jase frowned. "Yes. You're my sister."

He said the words with such certainty, it made Sienna's chest tighten. "I can picture the night we left," she told him. "I remember turning around in the back seat and watching you get smaller, then disappear in the darkness as Mom drove away." She shook her head. "But nothing else in any detail."

"There wasn't much worth remembering," Jase said with a small laugh.

"It was the first seven years of my life," Sienna countered. "And it's all a jumble to me."

"Is that part of what upsets you?" He studied her, his gaze intense, and a whisper of familiarity brushed over her like the touch of a feather. She could see in her mind the image of a solemn boy putting a bandage on her knee as she wiped away tears after a fall.

"I think so," she admitted. "Although I didn't realize I cared until I came to Colorado. Did you teach me to ride a bike?"

"Maybe you remember more than you think," Jase said.

"Here's the wine," Cole said as he came through the front door. "Everything okay?"

He pressed his fingers to the small of Sienna's back, handing Jase the bottle of wine. The light touch was more comforting than she could have imagined.

"It's fine," she said.

"Come into the kitchen," Jase told them both. "We'll eat soon."

Cole kept his hand on her back as they walked, reminding Sienna that she didn't have the option to run away, even if her hammering heart told her that would be the smart thing to do.

She heard voices and laughter as they walked toward the back of the house, but silence descended over the group as she entered the bright and airy kitchen.

Jase and Emily's house was an old Victorian, but the inside had been remodeled recently. The kitchen had white craftsman-style cabinets with dark soapstone countertops over them. The floors looked original in a deep mahogany stain. There was a vase of fresh flowers on the island and framed photos and kids art decorated the walls.

Emily, Katie and a friendly looking man who Sienna guessed was Noah Crawford all glanced between her and Cole, but it was Declan Crenshaw who moved forward.

"Isn't she the spitting image of your mother back in the day?" he asked Jase. "She even has Dana's eyes." He stopped when he was directly in front of Sienna. "You gonna take off again if I talk to you tonight?"

She shook her head, ignoring her sweaty palms and pounding heart.

"Good," he said, "because I got plenty to say."

"Dad, let's eat first." Jase's voice was gentle.

"It's been twenty years," Declan argued. "Food can wait."

"I'm hungry now," a small voice said from behind Sienna.

A young boy scooted past, keeping his hands at his sides so he wouldn't brush against her. A fluffy dog followed, wagging its tail and sniffing at Sienna and Cole before trotting forward to greet everyone else.

"Davey, we have people here for dinner," Emily said.

"I know," the boy answered, glancing at his mother before dropping his gaze back to the ground. He held out one hand and the dog immediately moved to his side, tucking herself against his leg. "I want a hot dog."

"Dogs and burgers are almost ready to come off the grill," Noah said. "I just checked them."

Jase touched Davey's shoulder. "Do you want to say hello to our guest?"

"Hi," the boy muttered but didn't make eye contact.

Everyone else seemed to take the behavior in stride.

Katie and Noah both greeted Davey and the adorable baby Noah held smiled widely.

Paige had told Sienna that Emily's son from a previous marriage had Asperger's, which explained the way he interacted with everyone. She looked toward Emily, who lifted her chin as if in challenge. Clearly, Jase's wife had been through some battles defending her boy.

Sienna didn't have much experience with kids, and certainly not special needs children, but she felt a new respect for Emily. "Why don't we talk over dinner?" she said to Declan. "Davey's not the only one who's ready to eat."

She saw Emily let out a breath, and Jase gave her an approving nod. "Davey, get a plate from your mommy," he told the boy, setting the wine on the counter, "and you can help me with the burgers and hot dogs."

"I'm Noah Crawford," Katie's husband said as he stepped forward. "This is little Willow."

"Nice to meet you," Sienna said, smiling.

She could feel her father's intense gaze on her and was relieved when Cole turned and engaged Declan in conversation. Emily handed Sienna a bowl of salad across the counter. "Would you bring this to the patio?"

"Sure." The nerves in Sienna's stomach began to settle slightly. Other than her dad's behavior, the evening felt almost normal. Better than normal even. Most of the social events she attended, even the casual summer get-togethers, involved catered food, cloth napkins and usually some kind of dress code. "No formal seating chart, right?" she asked Katie as they stepped outside.

Katie chuckled. "You really did grow up a world away from Crimson."

They took seats around the wrought-iron table on the large patio that overlooked a lovely yard with a swing set in one corner. Sienna made sure she was at the opposite end from Declan. Something about the way he kept staring at her, like she was a ghost, made her uncomfortable. She'd come to Crimson to face her past but hadn't considered the fact that her dad might have his own ideas about their relationship.

She'd assumed he wouldn't care about seeing her. That she could say her piece, once she figured out what it was, then leave again and return to her old life or start creating a new one, since a big part of who she'd been was the next Mrs. Kevin Patterson.

She didn't have to say much during the meal. The others fell into an easy discussion about the upcoming July Fourth celebration in town and how elaborate the fireworks display over Crimson Mountain was going to be this year.

Sienna forced a smile at the same time she suppressed a shudder. She'd never liked fireworks. The high-pitched whistle and reverberating boom that followed made her edgy, heart hammering and breath coming in shallow pants like she was some kind of scared animal or soldier back from the front lines.

Her reaction had been a constant embarrassment to her mother. Each year, their country club hosted a big Fourth of July soiree, where everyone dressed in patriotic shades of red, white and blue, and the annual member photo would be displayed on the wall of the clubhouse. It was a point of pride for Sienna's mother that Craig's family had been one of the founding members of the club, which meant that the Pierces were guaranteed a front-row seat for the evening fireworks display, always spectacular and set to classical music.

The first year they'd attended, Sienna had puked all over the manicured lawn when her mother refused to excuse her as the display started. After that, it had been a battle of wills each summer and Sienna's fear of the noise and scent of sulfur had only increased.

"You remember," Declan shouted suddenly, pointing a bony finger at Sienna. "And it still gets to you."

All eyes turned to Sienna, other than Davey, who continued to pet Ruby, sitting loyally next to his chair.

Sienna swallowed. "I don't know what you mean."

"Dad, calm down." Jase shifted in his chair and put a hand out in what Sienna guessed was an attempt to quiet Declan.

But the older man shook him off, rising from the table and moving toward Sienna. Cole stood, as well, like he was ready to protect her if needed.

"Sit down, Declan," Cole said in a serious law enforcement tone. It sounded to Sienna like the sheriff had some experience with her father acting out.

"Turn your wrist over," Declan commanded, ignoring Cole. Sienna obeyed automatically. She hated that her first instinct was to obey without question, even though Cole had called her a rebel. What a joke.

"Don't touch her." Cole blocked Declan when the older man reached for Sienna.

"He's not going to hurt her," Jase said, frustration lacing his tone.

"What's for dessert?" Davey asked solemnly.

"In a minute, honey," Emily told him.

The questions and comments swirling around Sienna sounded distant and muffled, as if they were coming through a tunnel. She was alone on the other end, her attention focused on the crescent-shaped scar on the inside of her arm, just to the right of the center of her wrist. It had been there since she could remember and had grown so faint over the years she'd all but forgotten it.

But as her father stared at the same spot, a memory flickered to life in the back of her mind. Like a flame exposed to air, it grew. She saw herself as a young girl, sticky with cotton candy at a summer carnival with the massive outline of Crimson Mountain as a backdrop.

She held a sparkling wand in her hand, making big circles in the air and laughing at the trail of light and smoke her movements made. Her brother was next to her and a dozen more kids all around them. Suddenly a whistle and a thunderous boom sounded. People around them clapped, but the noise startled Sienna and she let the sparkler drop to her other wrist, then screamed as the tip of it burned her skin.

Tears had come hot and fast, and Jase had called for someone. Sienna would have expected a younger Dana to be the one to rush over, but she could see her mother enraptured by the fireworks display as she laughed with her friends nearby. Instead, Declan peeled away from the crowd. He plucked the sparkler from her fingers, then hefted her into his arms.

"It's all right, baby girl," he told her. "It's just a wee burn." She buried her face in her daddy's shirtfront, which smelled of beer and cigarettes—an oddly comforting combination to her little-girl senses.

"Make the noise stop," she'd said in a whimper. "The boom makes it hurt worse."

He'd carried her to the beer tent and taken a piece of ice from one of the kegs to rub over her red skin. She kept her eyes shut tightly, unwilling to look at the fireworks she blamed for her pain.

Now she glanced up to Declan's knowing gaze. "You remember," he repeated quietly and she gave a jerky nod.

"Remember what?" Cole demanded.

"Sienna got burned by a sparkler when she was little,"

Jase said before she had a chance to answer. "She never liked fireworks after that."

It shouldn't be a surprise that Jase could recount the story as easily as Sienna. He'd been the one to call for help. But the fact that her brother and father seemed to know more details of her early life than she could remember rocked her to her core just the same.

"I've got to go." Sienna pushed back from the table. "Thank you for dinner, Emily." She forced herself to smile as she glanced around the table. "Thanks to all of you for making me feel welcome."

She turned away and hurried into the house before anyone could stop her. Her biggest fear was that her dad would follow, forcing her to pull up more memories. Not that remembering the night she'd been burned was painful exactly, but she'd always told herself that neither Declan or Jase cared about her at all—that's the reason they let her go.

She'd never questioned why her early childhood memories were somewhat blank in her brain. She figured there was nothing good to remember about the years she'd lived in Crimson.

But she was quickly coming to realize that wasn't true. That knowledge seemed to change everything.

Chapter Ten

Cole turned his truck off the road and rolled down the windows, gravel crunching under the tires as he pulled to a stop at the edge of the trees.

"Where are we?" Sienna asked, blinking like she was waking up from a dream. She'd been in her own world since they left Jase and Emily's, staring out the front window while she rubbed a finger over the tiny scar on her wrist.

They hadn't spoken because she seemed to need quiet and Cole respected that. He understood the need to process things and didn't want to push her too hard or fast. But he also wasn't willing to let her go just yet.

She might not realize it, but alone was the last thing Sienna needed to be at the moment.

"One of my favorite spots in Crimson." He turned off the truck and opened his door. "Come on."

"I should go home," she protested weakly.

He glanced over his shoulder, arching a brow in her direction. "Where is home for you right now?" he asked, not to be unkind but because he was truly curious how she would answer.

She tugged her bottom lip between her teeth and sucked in a breath. "Fine," she said after a moment, not answering his question. "Show me this special spot of yours."

He led her down the dirt path, holding back branches that hung across the trail, partially obstructing it and hiding it from plain sight. It was one of the things Cole liked best about this area—not many people knew it existed so even at the height of summer tourist season, it wasn't crowded.

The sun was just beginning to dip behind the peak, the evening light that played through the trees soft and warm.

"Watch your step," he told her as they navigated a rocky section of the trail.

A minute later, the forest ended and they emerged onto a grassy knoll with the river flowing in front of them. From the spot they were standing, there was a view of the tip of Crimson Mountain in the distance, along with a hillside covered in aspen trees and early season wildflowers on the other side of the bank.

"It's beautiful," Sienna whispered.

The look of wonder playing across her face was far more to Cole's liking than the confusion and pain in her gaze right before she'd rushed from the table at Jase's.

His heart skipped a beat, and he smiled. "The river is high right now because of runoff from the snow. It will be half this size by August if we have another dry summer."

"Look, there's deer over there." Sienna pointed to a spot in front of the trees near the bend in the river. "Those are the biggest deer I've ever seen."

"Because they're elk," Cole explained. "They come

down to the river this time of day. They'll go back up to higher ground as the weather gets warmer."

He stepped back and pointed to a bench tucked at the base of two pine trees about ten feet away. "Want to sit down?"

Sienna glanced between him and the rustic wooden bench. "Did you build that?"

"I wish I had that talent," he said, shaking his head as they moved toward the trees. "I found out about this place from one of the guys who ran the snowplow when I first got a job with the sheriff's department. Manny's retired now and moved to Pueblo last year to be closer to his daughter. He and his wife used to come out here so he could fish." Cole brushed a few pine needles off the bench, then took a seat next to Sienna on it. "He built this so his wife would have a comfortable place to sit and read while he did his thing."

"That's sweet," Sienna murmured.

"Yeah. There's a few popular fishing spots about a half mile down on either side, but not many people come right here because the trailhead isn't obvious."

"Do you fish?" she asked.

"Not nearly as much as I'd like," he admitted. He pointed to a section of the river where the current wasn't running so hard. "But that's about as perfect of a spot as you can get."

"My dad used to fish. I remember it now."

Sienna was back to worrying the tip of one finger against the scar on her wrist.

"He still does." Cole took her hand in his, lacing their fingers together. "Want to talk about earlier?"

"No."

He lifted her hand and grazed a kiss over her knuckles. "Talk to me anyway."

"I made them into the bad guys," she said after a moment. "They were the ones who didn't want me then. They wouldn't want me now." She swiped at her cheek with the hand he wasn't holding. "I never questioned why I couldn't remember any details from the time before Mom and I left Crimson. She'd barely talk about it or her reasons for leaving, so I think I made up a story in my mind about how bad it was."

"And maybe that wasn't the whole story?"

She looked over at him. "It wasn't great. My memories are hazy but coming back to me. You may not have been raised here, but you've heard plenty of Crenshaw stories, I'm sure."

"Yeah," he admitted. "The family track record is spotty at best."

"The Crenshaw track record is a mess of crater-size potholes and everyone knows it. I thought there was nothing more to my father. I wanted closure. I wanted him to admit that he didn't care enough to make my mom stay. He didn't fight or come after me."

She shook her head, and a lock of blond hair fell forward against her cheek. "If you'd asked me a week ago, I would have told you there was nothing Declan Crenshaw or even Jase could say that would make me forgive them for letting her take me."

"Even though your life might have been better away from here. The advantages and opportunities you had—"

"But it wasn't my life." She pulled her hand away from his, stood and paced to the edge of the river. He let her go, watched as she hugged her arms around herself. There were some things a person had to work out on their own, and Cole hoped the serenity of this space—the view of the mountains surrounding them and the sound of the river babbling over rocks—would help her calm the demons pulling at her.

He'd certainly come here often enough to soothe his own soul.

She turned back to him after a few minutes. "I know I sound like an ungrateful little princess," she said, her gaze pained. "I did have opportunities. I had stability and security. They sent me to the right schools and ballet and debutante balls. I went to cotillion and birthday parties where parents rented ponies and magicians and we vacationed to beaches and mountains and…"

She threw up her hands. "None of it mattered because it wasn't mine. My mom made the choice to reinvent herself, and she worked so hard to leave behind everything about her marriage and life before. But I was always there, a physical reminder of the mistakes she'd made."

"She couldn't have thought of you as a mistake," Cole argued, hating that she believed that about herself. "She's your mother."

Sienna gave a sharp bark of laughter. "Not all moms are created equal, Sheriff. It wasn't that I blamed her. I didn't think she had a choice. She made me think that. Now I know…"

She sat down again beside him. "Somehow I blocked the details before we left. But I remember…not all of it but enough. She left Jase behind because Dad needed him. He was always the strong one—the caretaker of all of us. I wasn't that important, so I got the ticket out of Crimson."

She held up her wrist, pale and delicate in the soft evening light. "I dropped a sparkler on myself at one of the Crimson Fourth of July festivals. Maybe I was five at the time. My dad took care of me. Granted, he got ice from a beer keg plus a refill at the same time, but he tried to make it better."

"Declan isn't a bad man," Cole told her. "He has issues, but he's also got a big heart."

"I wanted—needed—him to be the bad guy in this." She leaned forward and placed her elbows on her knees. "My brother taught me how to ride a bike. He sat with me instead of his friends on the bus home from school when I started kindergarten so I wouldn't get scared."

"You didn't remember any of this before tonight?"

"No. The only things Mom would ever discuss were the drinking and fighting between her and my dad. So those are the things I remember. Now I wonder which are mine and which are hers."

"I'm sorry, Sienna." He curled his fingers around her neck and massaged gently.

"But that doesn't give me an answer to the million-dollar question. Why did my dad let me go so easily?" She swayed toward him, and Cole looped an arm around her shoulder and pulled her close.

"I don't know, sweetheart. You'll have to ask him."

"I'm so afraid," she whispered, "of hearing the answer." She let out a choked sob that just about ripped open Cole's chest. He pressed a long kiss to the top of her head and smoothed a hand over her hair.

After a few minutes, she straightened, dabbed her fingers to the corners of her eyes and shifted to face him. "How did you lose your parents?" she asked, and he felt his head snap back like she'd punched him.

"We were talking about your messed-up family," he said, trying to keep his tone light. "Not mine."

"Change of subject."

He swallowed, ignoring the tightening in his gut. He hated revisiting his past. Most people were shocked enough when he shared that his family had died that he could sidestep giving any details. Leave it to Sienna to be different.

"My father killed himself," he said bluntly. "Mom had a heart attack six months later." He closed his eyes and added, "I'm pretty sure she actually died of a broken heart."

"Oh, Cole. Was your father… Did he… Were there drugs or alcohol involved?"

"Not a bit."

"Mental illness?"

He shook his head, feeling the suffocating band of anger and humiliation tighten around him. "He was a career army man, close to retirement age. They were based outside of DC at the time. My mom had her eye on an RV. She'd traveled the world but wanted to see the United States."

"That's sweet."

"Yeah," he agreed. "She was a sweetheart. The perfect army wife. She could make the most basic military housing feel like home. Then my dad was arrested."

"For what?"

"He was charged with conspiracy and bribery. There was a ring of officers being bribed by a defense contractor in the Middle East. They gave him classified and confidential information that he used to defraud the US military and he offered…" Cole paused, shook his head "…a lot of things in return. Apparently it had been going on for years, and he was one of the ringleaders. He denied everything, but the government had enough evidence."

Sienna placed a hand on his leg. His skin burned beneath the fabric of his jeans where the warmth of her seeped through.

"Mom posted bail, and he came home. The next week, he shot himself."

"No," Sienna whispered. "Did she—?"

"I found him," he said. "Mom had asked my brother and me to fly in. She thought seeing the two of us would bolster his spirits. She'd come to pick me up at the airport. Shep was arriving that night. There was a note on the door when we got back to the house that I should come in without her."

"I can't even imagine, Cole. I'm so sorry."

He shrugged, trying to stay strong. He'd become immune to sympathy in the weeks following his father's death because at that time the kind remarks were always laced with a trace of judgment.

Almost everyone in his parents' circle of friends was or had been military at some point. The accusations against his father, and the fact that his suicide seemed tantamount to admitting guilt, were a hard pill to swallow for some people. Most people.

The question of the kind of man his father truly was had driven a wedge between Cole and his twin. Shep had always been a free spirit, the family rebel and the brother who'd given their parents the most trouble growing up. He'd felt somehow justified in his choices after Richard Bennett's years of treachery had been revealed.

Cole, who at the time was stationed in Texas, proud to follow in his father's footsteps with his own military career, had been knocked so far off center he wasn't sure he'd ever right himself again. Despite the mountain of evidence, including emails and other correspondence that implicated Colonel Bennett, Cole still wanted to believe his dad could be innocent.

"The worst was mom's reaction," Cole told her, keeping his voice neutral as emotions buffeted him from every side. "She was his biggest supporter. She'd been so proud of his service. Even after the arrest, she insisted he'd been framed. She wanted him to be the honorable man she'd married but would have stood by his side no matter the outcome."

"He didn't give her that choice," Sienna said quietly.

"She felt like he'd abandoned her. It didn't help that Shep was doing the 'I told you so' routine every waking minute. Her pain didn't seem to phase him at all."

She squeezed his leg. "That couldn't have gone over well with you. It's obvious you were protective of your mom."

"Picture the most generous, selfless, caring person you can imagine, then multiply by ten. That was my mom."

"You were lucky."

"So was Shep. I still don't get how we could have had the same parents, the same childhood, most of the same experiences and his take on everything was the polar opposite of mine."

"I can't answer that," Sienna said. "Jase and I obviously had different upbringings, at least for most of it. Did you finally get your brother to come around?"

Cole shook his head. "We got in a fight at Dad's funeral. Both of us ended up with black eyes, and he had a split lip to go with it. Never could block a shot. Mom blamed us both." He closed his eyes as memory and regret coalesced inside his chest. "Shep left that night. I haven't talked to him since."

"What about when your mom died?" Sienna asked.

He pressed his lips together, then said, "He didn't come back, and I did a private burial. Without Shep, it was only me there. I couldn't stand the idea of her family and friends judging her in death at a big service."

"You don't know—"

"I do," he insisted. "It was awful for her, and she had no one with Dad gone."

"She had you."

He stood, paced a few steps forward and plucked a stone from the creek bank, hurling it toward the river. It skipped across the water twice, then disappeared into the current with a plop.

He closed his eyes and listened to the water, hoping the bubbling sound would calm his tumultuous emotions as it had so many other evenings. This was the place he came when he needed to regroup—when the stress of work or the sting of the past got to be too much.

Before tonight, he'd always come here alone.

He felt more than heard Sienna come up behind him. She wrapped her arms around his waist and pressed her cheek to the center of his back. "Neither one of our fathers fought for us," she said into his shirt. "What a pair."

A pair.

Cole liked the sound of that. He liked the thought of not being alone, and especially of not being alone with Sienna. She softened his edges, dulling the throbbing pain inside his heart until it lessened to a manageable ache.

No one had ever been able to reach him that way before. Cole might be stubborn, but he wasn't stupid. What she gave to him was precious, a gift to be cherished even if only for a short time.

So he turned around, cupped her cheeks between his hands and kissed her.

Chapter Eleven

A tremor raced along Sienna's skin at the press of Cole's mouth to hers. Within seconds, he deepened the kiss, his tongue lacing with hers and their breath mingling until she wasn't sure where he ended and she began.

The emotions that assailed her from tonight still held on, but being with Cole had loosened their grip on her. They were distant now, brushing against her legs like tall grass in a summer field instead of making her feel like she was being sucked down into suffocating quicksand.

The longer they kissed, the more she lost herself in the moment—in the feel of Cole's strong body against hers, the way he held her face so tenderly.

It was as if he saw her for something more than she knew herself to be. Someone who could handle whatever life threw at her, even though she had so many doubts about herself. He'd trusted her with his own painful memories, and she had a suspicion that wasn't something he did lightly.

"Let's go..." She paused because what she wanted to say was "home" but she didn't have a home at the moment. Yes, her condo was waiting for her back in Chicago but the idea of returning there now felt foreign to her. She no longer belonged in her own life, but she didn't quite have a place in Crimson either. The Bumblebee was lovely, but only a temporary situation. Everything felt fleeting at the moment, and she desperately wanted to hold on to something sure.

"To my place?" Cole whispered against her mouth, and she nodded.

Not her home, but it would do for now.

He took her hand and they returned down the path toward the parking lot. Shadows fell over the trail and the air had already cooled several degrees.

A shiver passed through her as she climbed into the truck, and she wished she'd worn more to dinner than a thin T-shirt with her jeans. As if reading her mind, Cole reached into the back seat, then handed her a fleece pullover.

"This should help," he said as he turned the key in the ignition.

"I'm fine," she lied. It was obvious she was nowhere near fine. She slipped the soft fabric over her head, inhaling the scent of laundry soap and spice she would forever associate with her sexy sheriff.

Her sheriff.

Heart stuttering at that thought, she zipped up the fleece. Cole might not be hers forever, but she wasn't going to waste this chance with him.

"Do you want seat heat?" he asked.

She shook her head. "The jacket is plenty. Do you mind if I roll down my window?"

He gave her a confused glance out of the corner of his eye. "I saw you shiver."

"I'm warm now, and I love the smell of the forest." She paused, then added, "I love the scent of pine. I didn't remember it until tonight, but there were woods at the edge of the trailer park where we lived. I used to build forts and secret hideaways in the trees. Sometimes when my mom and dad fought, I'd escape and pretend I lived in the woods by myself."

He depressed both of the window buttons, and a moment later cool air and the crisp scent of pine filled the truck. Sienna leaned back against the headrest and let her eyes drift closed. She was used to the hot, humid air of Midwestern summers and appreciated the freshness of the mountains in a way she couldn't have guessed before returning to Crimson.

"Actually," she said softly, glancing over at Cole, "an escape still sounds like a pretty good idea."

He chuckled and took her hand, enfolding it in his larger one. They didn't speak the rest of the drive back into town. Now that she was calmer, Sienna had a chance to process everything that had happened tonight and what she was about to do with Cole.

What going to his house with him meant. Nerves skittered along her skin, but she didn't consider changing her mind. She wanted him and for once she wasn't going to waste time second-guessing herself.

He parked the car in the driveway and came around to open her door. "I'm happy you're here," he said and leaned in to kiss her.

"Your neighbors might see," she said against his mouth, then pulled back.

"I don't want to hide anything."

She gave his arm a playful nudge as they walked toward the house. "Is the beloved town sheriff really allowed to bring a woman home for the night?"

They entered the house, cool and quiet in the evening light. "This is nobody's business but ours," he said, dumping his keys onto a table next to the door.

She liked the sound of that—of having something here in Crimson that belonged only to her. It was doubtful Cole truly meant the words, but she still appreciated them.

She wrapped her arms around his neck and kissed him, letting everything else melt away in the heat of her desire. The kiss was slow and deep but quickly turned molten. Suddenly she couldn't wait any longer. There was nothing Sienna needed more than Cole—all of him with every part of her.

As if sensing the change in her, the consuming need pulsing through her, he lifted her into his arms. She held on tight, her legs encircling his hips as he moved from the family room down the hall.

He continued to kiss her as he moved, and she smiled against his mouth. "A man who can multitask. I like it."

"I aim to please," he told her, rounding the corner of what was obviously his bedroom. In the soft light coming from the window, she could see that the walls were painted pale gray and the furniture was dark wood, heavy and masculine. Perfect for Cole.

He pulled back the sheets and followed her down onto the mattress.

"Too many clothes." She pushed at his wide shoulders.

He laughed softly. "I thought we'd try a little foreplay first."

"Foreplay later," she countered. "Right now I need you." She leveled a look at him, hoping he'd get the message. "Right. Now."

Straightening, he flipped on the light next to the bed, then tugged his shirt over his head, revealing a broad, muscled chest that made her mouth go dry. The hard planes weren't a surprise, but the sight of his golden skin and the smattering of dark hair across his chest were the sexiest things she'd ever seen.

"Your pants, too," she demanded, pointing a finger at him.

One side of his mouth curved. "Do you want to check and make sure my butt passes the no-sag test?"

She shook her head. "I have no concerns about your butt."

His grin widened. "I hope you're not going to make me get naked alone." One finger traced the top button of his jeans. "I could move a lot faster with the right motivation."

Sienna wasn't totally inexperienced with men, but she couldn't remember a time when she'd had so much fun in the bedroom. And they hadn't even gotten to the good part yet.

She sat up, then undid the buttons on her cotton shirt. The soft fabric tickled her overly sensitive skin as it fell from her arms. She looked down at herself, then said a silent prayer of thanks that she'd worn a pretty bra tonight.

Reaching behind her back, she unfastened it and tugged the red straps off her shoulders.

"Is this what you had in mind?"

Cole's eyes had gone as dark as rich chocolate. His chest rose and fell like he was having trouble catching his breath. "I couldn't have imagined you in my wildest dreams."

The hoarse rasp of his voice sent another round of shivers skittering over her skin. She liked the power she felt in this moment, reveled in his reaction to her.

"Then you're going to love this," she told him and tossed the lacy bra in his direction.

In what seemed like one fluid movement, he caught

it, tossed it aside and was stretched across her a moment later.

She gasped as his big hands covered her breasts, then arched into him when he captured one nipple in his mouth.

"So damn beautiful," he said and turned his attention to the other breast. Sensation spiked through her, making it feel like her whole body had gone liquid.

"I thought we agreed…" she paused to suck in a breath as his teeth grazed the tip of one breast "…to skip foreplay."

"This is too important," he said, then lifted his head. "You're too important to skip any part of it."

Emotion swept through her, even more overwhelming than the physical pleasure Cole was giving her. She raked her fingers through his hair, groaning when he shifted on the bed and undid her jeans, then tugged them, along with her panties, over her hips.

He straightened from the bed and undid his jeans, pushing them down and revealing himself to her. He was perfect…everywhere.

"Do you have…?" She glanced toward the nightstand.

"Yeah." The one word did crazy things to her body. How was it possible to feel so much when he'd barely touched her?

He stepped forward, opened the nightstand drawer and pulled out a condom, tearing open the wrapper with his teeth.

Automatically, Sienna reached for the light.

"Leave it on," Cole told her. "I want to see you."

He was on the bed a moment later, a perfect fit as he joined himself with her. She sucked in a breath as he entered her, wrapping her legs around his lean hips.

They moved together, slowly at first, the rhythm building as he kissed her like his life depended on it.

"You're perfect," he whispered, trailing kisses along her jaw.

"Hardly," she couldn't help but respond.

He stilled, and she could feel the tension in his body. "Perfect," he repeated, his gaze intense on hers.

She reached up and pulled his head down to hers, kissing him with all the emotion she wasn't willing to let him see in her eyes quite yet.

Pressure built inside her as they found a rhythm again and for the moment she let herself believe that she was perfect. That her life wasn't a total mess. She gave herself over to Cole and as soon as she did, it was like a million stars burst inside her.

She called out his name as pleasure washed over her, lifting her on a wave of sensation so strong it felt like she might never recover.

And in that instant, she realized she wouldn't recover from Cole Bennett. Because as much as she wanted to believe what was happening between them was just physical, to Sienna it was so much more.

His body tensed and he whispered her name like it was a prayer. After they'd both returned to earth, he held her tight, rolling over and taking her with him.

"Don't go anywhere," he told her like he thought she was some kind of flight risk.

Which could be the truth if she wasn't so boneless.

He took care of the condom, then returned to the bed, straightening the sheet and comforter over her and pulling her to his chest again.

"Perfect," he repeated, his tone gentle.

"Perfect," she agreed and let her eyes drift closed.

* * *

"Is it called the walk of shame even if you drove home?"

Sienna gasped and whirled around to find Paige leaning against the hallway doorframe.

"You practically scared the pants off me," Sienna said, clasping a hand to her chest.

Paige flashed a wide grin. "I think Cole took care of that last night."

Color rose to Sienna's cheeks and she forced herself not to look away. "No drive of shame this morning. I'm tired but not ashamed."

"Because you're so happy and satisfied?" Paige suggested. "Am I going to get all the naughty details?"

Sienna shook her head.

Paige made a face. "At least give me something. It's been a marathon dry spell around here. I need to live vicariously through someone."

"It was nice," Sienna said. "Now I need coffee. Do I smell banana bread?"

"Yes," Paige said, walking down the hall toward the kitchen with Sienna following. "But you can only have a piece if you tell me last night was the most amazing, life-changing experience you've ever had." She grabbed a mug from the counter and handed it to Sienna. "And that Sheriff Bennett is as thorough and capable as I'd imagine."

Sienna took the mug and moved toward the coffeepot.

"In case we haven't discussed it," Paige told her, "I have a very vivid imagination."

Sienna had a difficult time hiding her grin. "Yes."

"Yes?"

She kept her gaze on the mug as she poured coffee in it. "To all of it. Amazing, life changing, thorough and capable doesn't do him justice."

Paige squealed and did a little dance, coffee sloshing over the mug she held. "I knew it."

"That's all I'm going to say," Sienna added quickly. "No details."

"Fine," Paige said as she grabbed a paper towel from the rack attached to the underside of the cabinet. "I even kind of respect you for it. Although I wouldn't complain if you changed your mind."

Sienna shook her head. "What's going on around here?" She gestured toward the living room, where there was still a gaping hole in the floor.

"The contractor is coming today to tell me how much money I don't have that it will take to fix everything."

"Sorry."

Paige shrugged. "I'll figure it out. I always do. What's next for you and Cole?"

"Nothing."

"Do we need to revisit amazing, thorough and more than capable?"

"It was great but I'm not here for that. I need to talk to my dad. We had a little incident last night."

"What does that mean?"

"I never remembered much about my life before we left Crimson. I'm starting to now. It's weird. The situation was so black-and-white to me, but there's more to it than I realized."

"There always is with family."

Sienna sipped at her coffee. "Do you need help with money for the repairs? I have some savings that—"

"No." Paige held up a hand. "You're a guest here—my only paying guest at the moment."

"That's not going to change," Sienna pointed out, "until the inn is up and running. Isn't summer the big tourist season in town?"

"Well, yes."

"So you need to get things moving."

"Are you trying to manage my life because it's easier to deal with than yours?"

Sienna sighed. "Maybe."

Paige sliced a piece of banana bread from the loaf cooling on the stove, placed it on a small plate and handed it to Sienna. "Eat some carbs, then go visit Declan. I'll let you know when I need help around here."

"Fine." Sienna popped a bite of the sweet bread in her mouth, then headed upstairs for a shower. The part of her night with Cole she hadn't shared was the fact that she'd rushed to get dressed and run out of his house while he was showering this morning. It was cowardly and stupid, but as close as she'd felt to him last night, she couldn't quite face him in the morning. There were way too many questions about where they went next that she wasn't ready to ask or to answer.

She got dressed in the clothes she'd worn her first day in Colorado—a silk shirt and pleated trousers far too formal for this town. She really needed to shop for something new, but that was one more item on her to-do list she was embarrassed to admit she couldn't handle at the moment.

Did she buy clothes appropriate for summer in Colorado or restock her wardrobe with items she'd be able to use back in her old life? It was hard to know when she was so unclear as to what was coming next.

She could hear Paige talking to someone when she came back downstairs and noticed an enormous truck parked at the curb with the words Travers Construction painted on the side.

Sienna slipped out the front door and headed for her

rental car. Her phone rang just as she turned the key in the ignition.

"Did you forget something?" Cole's deep voice asked when she picked up.

She swallowed, butterflies taking flight in her belly just at the sound of his voice. "I don't think so."

"How about to say goodbye?" he suggested, and she could hear both amusement and frustration lacing his tone.

"You were in the shower."

"The bathroom door wasn't locked."

"Oh."

"Thank you for staying with me," he said gently. "Next time don't run off."

"Oh," she repeated, realizing she sounded like an idiot but unable to form better words.

"There *will* be a next time," Cole told her, once again displaying his uncanny ability to read her mind."

She licked her dry lips. "Okay."

He chuckled. "What are your plans today?"

"I'm going to see my dad. After last night, there are things he and I need to talk about."

"Memories?"

"I know my mom's side of the story." Sienna pushed her hair away from her face. "Why she left and why she took me and not Jase. I want to understand Declan's side."

"And?" Cole prompted.

"Why he never reached out to me," Sienna admitted.

"You have a right to answers."

"Thank you," she whispered. "I'll call you later."

She disconnected the call, took a deep breath and drove to her father's neighborhood on the other side of downtown.

It was another beautiful day in Crimson, the bright sun warming the air. The sky overhead was the brilliant blue she was quickly coming to associate with Colorado, and she realized now why she'd never quite grown accustomed to the gray skies that hung over Chicago at different times during the year. Some place inside her remembered the expansive swath of blue and the constant sun, because the warmth of the rays felt like a hug from a long-lost friend.

She didn't stop at Life is Sweet this morning, keeping her focus on her goal of meeting with Declan. Downtown was just beginning to wake up as she drove through, and she wondered if Jase was already at his office or still at home.

Did he find it as crazy as she did that she barely remembered anything about the first seven years of her life? He'd seemed shocked at her reaction to the talk about fireworks. Maybe if things went well with her father, she'd go and see Jase next.

Maybe today would be the day she'd get closure on issues that had plagued her for decades. Maybe today she could finally move forward.

She got out of the car as soon as she parked, not letting her nerves get the better of her.

Declan opened the front door as she approached. He wore a black T-Shirt and faded Levis. So different from her stepfather, who favored monogrammed button-downs and crisp cotton pants even on the weekends. "I wondered if I'd see you this morning," he said, stepping back to let her into the space. "I wasn't sure after you took off last night."

"I didn't remember how I got the scar on my wrist," she admitted as she walked past him. "When I did, it threw me for a loop."

She blinked several times as she took in the interior of the small family room, her breath catching in her throat.

"Is that the same sofa you had in the trailer?" she asked in a whisper.

Declan let out a small laugh behind her. "That throwing you for a loop, too?"

"Maybe."

Definitely. She walked forward and placed a hand on the back of the worn fabric, a heavy plaid pattern that was faded and threadbare in some spots.

"Jase wanted me to get something new, but this is the most comfortable couch I've ever sat on. Besides, it's lucky."

"How do you figure?"

"I watched the Broncos win two Super Bowl rings on that couch. Look at this." He moved around to the front of the sofa and picked up one of the cushions, holding it up so she could see the underside of it. "See that stain?"

Sienna stifled a grimace. "Yes."

"You had reflux as baby," he told her with a grin. "Seemed like you threw up more formula than you kept down some days. That's from you."

"Oh." She had no idea how to respond to that or the pride in Declan's voice, like he should be awarded some kind of gold star for his knowledge of her.

"I understand things about you, baby girl." Her heart ached at the term of endearment. More memories whispered into her mind, hazy and fine like a wisp of smoke. She could make them out as if through a fog, smell them, taste the past on the tip of her tongue but if she reached for them, tried to hold them in her hands, they disappeared like mist.

In their place, anger rose like a wave inside her. "You don't know enough. You have this tiny scar, but Mom has the rest of me. She was the one who held back my hair when I got the flu and puked for three days."

She pressed a hand to her stomach. "Would you like to see the scar from when I had my appendix out senior year of high school? I sure don't remember you being in the hospital or sending a card."

"I didn't know," he said, placing the cushion back on the sofa.

"You don't know anything about me. Maybe you've convinced yourself you were a decent dad when I was young, but a good father wouldn't let his daughter go the way you did."

"Your mother didn't give me a choice," Declan argued, but his voice was weak, shaky.

"There's always a choice." Sienna paced to the far side of the room, drawn by the framed photographs displayed on the narrow bookshelf. One showed Emily's son, Davey, holding up a trout on a dock in front of a mountain lake. One was a photo of Declan and Jase that looked like it had been taken at that same lake.

The third was Sienna as a toddler. She wore a pale yellow dress with a pattern of sunflowers across the front of it and her blond hair was pulled back into two pigtails. It was a photo she hadn't seen before. Her mother didn't have many pictures of Sienna before they moved to Chicago.

"That was your favorite dress," her dad said from behind her. "You'd wear it for days at a time before your mom would force you to take it off so it could be washed."

Studying the photo was almost like looking at a stranger, even though she clearly recognized herself. She squeezed her eyes shut and combed through her memories, trying to recall the dress.

"It doesn't matter," she said after a moment, more to herself than Declan. "You let me go." She whirled around to face him. "Why didn't you fight for me? I can't imagine I was so precious to you if you didn't even come after me when Mom moved away."

"She needed you," he said, holding up his hands. "I knew there was no way to make her stay with how unhappy she was here. I loved your mother, but we were toxic together."

"All you needed was Jase," she said, the words like sandpaper scraping across her tongue. "As long as you had him—"

"He chose to stay," Declan argued. "Dana would have taken him, too, but—"

"He was a kid," Sienna shouted. "Just like me. Neither of you had the right to make the choice you did for either of us."

"Your mother was the one to cut off communication. This is her fault."

"You didn't fight for me." Sienna pounded an open palm against her chest. "Because I wasn't worth it to you."

"Not true." Declan ran a hand through his hair. "I thought about you every day. I loved you."

"Don't say that. You don't get to use those words with me." The emotion she'd kept at bay for so many years poured forth. The walls she'd built around her heart bursting open. She wanted to hurt her father the way she'd been hurt.

"This was a mistake," she said, drawing in a deep breath. "I have nothing to say to you because you mean nothing to me. Less than nothing." She bit down on her bottom lip to keep from crying. That's how his tacit rejection had made her feel—less than nothing. For years, she'd taken scraps of affection from everyone around her because that's all she felt like she deserved.

She started toward the front door. Fresh air and sunshine would remind her that there was a big world still spinning despite the pinpoint of her own problems that seemed to be all she could see at the moment.

Her fingers had just gripped the knob when the crash had her spinning back around. Her breath caught as she saw Declan land on the floor, eyes closed and body limp. The lamp and side table he'd knocked over during his fall lay on the ground next to him.

"Dad!" she screamed, already reaching for her cell phone to dial 911.

Chapter Twelve

Cole took off his hat as he strode through the automatic doors of Crimson Community Hospital an hour later.

He'd been out near the county line when Marlene had radioed him to report that Declan Crenshaw was being rushed to the ER.

Marlene told him Jase was already on his way to the hospital, so Cole tried calling Sienna's cell but hadn't been able to reach her. He'd called Paige next, and his gut twisted when she'd explained in a frantic voice that Sienna hadn't returned after the visit with her father that morning.

He couldn't imagine a scenario where Sienna might have anything to do with Declan's condition, but the idea still scared the hell out of him. The last thing she needed was to deal with a health crisis surrounding her dad.

He scanned the waiting room and saw Emily and Noah next to each other on a small leather sofa.

"What happened?" he asked, moving toward them. "Is Declan okay?"

Emily shook her head. "We don't know. The doctor is with him now. They let Jase go back, but they're running more tests." She put a hand on her belly. "It was definitely his heart, but we don't know how serious it is yet."

Noah placed a hand on his sister's shoulder. "The old man is tough."

"Not like he used to be," Emily countered. "He puts on a good front, but all those years of drinking have taken their toll."

Cole ran a hand through his hair and glanced around the waiting room as if he could produce answers to take away some of Emily's anxiety. She and Jase had been through enough in the past year. They should be getting ready to come to the hospital for the happiest of reasons, not something like this.

"Has anyone talked to Sienna?"

Noah's lips pressed into a thin line, and Emily let out a muttered curse. "She was with him at the time," she said, meeting Cole's gaze. Her pale blue eyes were icy. "She rode here with him in the ambulance—called Jase on the way. But we haven't seen her."

Noah snorted. "At this point, all we know is she took off."

"You can't blame her," Cole said immediately.

"Where is she then?" Noah asked. "As usual, Jase is left to take care of his dad on his own."

"I'll find her." Cole stepped away and punched in Sienna's cell number again. The call went straight to voice mail so he sent a text. When a response didn't come immediately, he approached the reception desk.

"Hey, Dixie," he said with a small smile for the fifty-something woman behind the computer.

"Howdy, Sheriff." The woman fluffed her hair as she

spoke. "Are you here checking on Declan? I hope it's not too serious, especially for Jase's sake. That boy has been through hell and back for his dad."

"Yeah," Cole agreed automatically. "I'm hoping you can help me with something. There was a woman who rode in the ambula—"

"The daughter," Dixie said in a scandalized whisper. "I'd heard she was back in town. Looks exactly like her mother did years ago. I used to see Dana Crenshaw in the grocery—do you remember that she was a checker down at the Shop & Go back in the day?"

"I don't," Cole admitted, mentally counting to ten. He'd learned quickly upon his arrival in Crimson that a small town moved at its own pace. Most people in Crimson were friendly to a fault, but they wouldn't be rushed in how they doled out their help.

"We all knew she'd taken a step back marrying Declan. It was obvious she didn't belong in that trailer park. Falling in love makes a woman do stupid things. She was half out of her mind most of the time, but sober she handled those groceries like she was the queen of England. People around here didn't see, but I knew she was destined for better things."

"You're a good woman, Dixie. As far as Sienn—"

"Do you think the daughter takes after her mom?" Dixie frowned, tapping a finger on her glossed lips. "It was hard to tell when they came through here. I gave her the paperwork to fill out for Declan, and she didn't say much. But the poor thing could have been in shock, you know? I remember when—"

"Have you seen her?" Cole interrupted, unable to be patient any longer. "I'm looking for Sienna."

"Well then." Dixie studied him for a few moments, her brows raised. "She might have headed for the cafeteria."

She pointed down the hall. "I think I mentioned that Tuesday is tomato soup day, since she was going to be waiting for her dad. People forget to eat in times of stress."

"Thanks, Dixie." Cole smiled again. "The hospital is lucky to have you."

"Of course they are," the woman agreed with a wink. "See you, Sheriff."

Cole glanced back to the waiting room, but Emily and Noah hadn't moved and Jase was still nowhere in sight. He made his way quickly to the cafeteria, scanning the tables until he saw a familiar cascade of blond hair near the far corner.

"Hey," he said as he came to stand next to her. "You doing okay?"

Sienna glanced up, then quickly away, her eyes round with what looked like residual shock. Her skin was pale, her shoulders slumped. Cole wanted nothing more than to gather her in his arms and tell her he'd make everything right again.

"I should never have come here," she told him, shaking her head.

"Don't say that." He pulled out the chair next to her, metal scraping against the floor.

"Why not? Everyone else will be." She stared directly in front of her, unwilling to look at him. "I could hear it in Jase's voice when I called him." She shuddered. "Do you know what he said? 'What did you do to him?' Like the cardiac arrest was my fault."

"It wasn't."

"You don't know that." She pressed a hand to her chest. "I don't know that. The woman at the front desk handed me all this paperwork like I can fill it out. As if I know anything about my father's medical history or insurance." She gave a short laugh. "I don't even know his birth date."

She grabbed the clipboard from the table, holding it so tight her knuckles turned white. Cole placed a hand over hers, willing her to relax.

"Look at me, Sienna. Tell me what happened."

She shook her head. "I went to his house, and we argued. Or I argued. I yelled at him. So much anger came tumbling out." Her gaze flicked to his. "He had a framed photo of me as a girl, and it set everything off. He thinks he knows me, but he doesn't. He couldn't possibly."

"You can change that."

"I've done a real bang-up job so far." She blew out a breath. "I spent my first week in town hiding out only to storm away from a family dinner. Then today—" Her voice cut out on a choked sob. "What if Declan doesn't make it? What if all those horrible things I said are his last memories of me?"

"It wouldn't matter." He lifted his free hand to the back of her neck, gently massaging the tight muscles there. "Declan owns his mistakes, and he made some big ones with you. That's on him, Sienna."

She leaned into his touch and let out a sigh. "How I deal with him now is on me. I'm an adult. I have a life. My daddy didn't want me when I was a girl. Big deal, right?"

Cole thought of his relationship with his own father. Until his arrest, Richard Bennett had been a picture-perfect parent. He'd taught Cole and Shep to fish and hunt, run alongside them when they'd learned to ride bikes. He'd been to every football game and parent-teacher conference he was in town for, and most of all he'd always made both boys feel safe and loved. At least that's how Cole had seen it. Shep had a different opinion—bristling against the strict rules his father set in the house.

Cole's dad had been his idol, which was why his arrest and then shocking death had hit so hard. He still couldn't imagine how he would have felt growing up without his dad or believing he didn't want anything to do with him.

"Come back with me to the waiting area. Emily and Noah are there while Jase is in the room with Declan."

"Saint Jase," Sienna muttered.

"No one blames you."

She rolled her eyes. "Liar."

"It won't help to keep yourself separate from them."

"It'll help me," she said, her voice breaking, "not deal with the fact that I may have just killed my estranged father."

"Don't say that."

She lowered her head, tears dripping onto the hospital paperwork.

His heart ached, but clearly sympathy wasn't helping. "I never took you for a coward." He cringed inwardly when her shoulders stiffened.

A moment later, she looked up, her eyes blazing. If she could have killed him with a look, he'd be long gone. She swiped at her eyes. "Is this reverse psychology?" she asked, her tone menacing.

"You have to face this thing," he said instead of answering. "Or run back to Mommy and Stepdaddy and your little insulated world of privilege and first-world problems."

She barked out a laugh. "First-world problems. That's a good one."

"Where are you going to find the next candidate for a country club husband since the last one couldn't keep it in his pants?"

"I don't need another candidate."

She was angry now, every inch of her radiating temper. It was better than seeing her broken. He could take anything but that. "Maybe you should go for more of a father figure. Someone older, probably divorced and looking for wifey number two. You can try to work out some of the daddy issues you're too scared to face with your real father."

"Low blow, Sheriff," she said on a hiss of breath. "And rich coming from the man who hasn't talked to his twin brother in years. I'm not the only one who's messed up around here."

"You have no idea, sweetheart," he agreed. Somehow Sienna had worked her way past his defenses, and it scared the hell out of him how much her happiness mattered. If only he had something real to offer her. "Unlike you, I'm content with my mess. You came here to fix yours. Do you have the guts to do it?"

"You're a terrible man." She grabbed the clipboard and rose from the table. "You might be excellent in bed, but dealing with your head games is not worth the effort."

He followed as she stalked from the cafeteria. "You're moving," he told her, "toward the waiting room."

"Because you're a manipulative, jerky…jerk."

He kept his features schooled when she glanced over at him. "I'll take that."

"They don't want me here," she whispered as they drew closer to the hospital's main entrance.

"You're stronger than you realize, Sienna, even when you have to be bullied into admitting it."

"I'm not going to thank you for being mean," she said under her breath.

"Will you go out with me on a real date to make it up to you?"

She stopped in her tracks, took a deep breath and narrowed her eyes. "First you're rude and now you're trying to distract me before I go in front of the firing squad?"

"Or I'm just asking you out," he suggested with a wink.

"Definitely distraction," she agreed, then walked toward Emily and Noah.

"Any news on Declan?" Sienna kept her shoulders straight as she looked from Emily to Noah, proud her voice didn't falter.

"Where have you been?" Emily demanded, crossing her arms over her chest. "We've been here almost an hour and haven't seen you once."

"I needed some time to collect myself." There was no point in trying to act like she hadn't been deeply affected by watching her father almost die.

She'd started CPR immediately and the EMTs had arrived within minutes. They'd used a defibrillator to shock his heart into beating normally again, but he hadn't regained consciousness during the ambulance ride. No one would answer any of her questions about his condition and he'd been whisked behind the large metal doors that separated the exam and operating rooms from the public part of the hospital.

She'd been left standing in front of the reception desk, alone and scared half out of her mind. A woman had shoved the clipboard of paperwork into her hands and Sienna had rushed off to the women's restroom, shutting herself in a stall while she sucked in gasping breaths, fear and guilt and adrenaline pumping through her veins.

Don't die. Don't die. Don't die.

That was the refrain in her head, even though she hadn't spoken the words out loud. She hadn't trusted her voice, hadn't wanted to admit—even to herself— how much she couldn't stand the thought of losing him.

Yes, she'd been angry and about to walk out, but she still cared. Far too much. She always had.

"The last we heard," Noah said gently, as if he understood how difficult this was for her, "your father is stable."

"Thanks for calling Jase right away," Emily added, pulling her purse off the chair next to her. "Have a seat. It makes the baby nervous to have you looming over her like that."

"I wasn't exactly looming."

Cole gave her a small nod as she sat down. "I'm going to see if I can get more information."

"I'll go with you," Noah said and jumped out of his chair like he thought his sister and Sienna might get into a catfight right there in the middle of the hospital waiting room.

"He has to be okay," Sienna whispered when she and Emily were alone.

"Yes," Emily agreed. She reached for the clipboard. "Want me to work on the information you didn't know?"

"That's pretty much all of it," Sienna said with a sigh. "I'm useless."

"You got him here." Emily shrugged as she began filling in the little boxes. "That counts."

"But Jase is with him now. He doesn't need me."

"I don't know why either of your parents let things happen the way they did." Emily placed a hand on her round belly. "I'd never cut my daughter off from her father, and if I tried, Jase would fight me every step of the way. It's not fair that Declan didn't fight for you."

Sienna swallowed. "Yeah."

"I was married before I came back to Crimson and reconnected with Jase." Emily hugged the clipboard to her chest. "My first husband couldn't handle being a dad to a child with special needs. When I left the East Coast, he went on with life like Davey and I never existed. He doesn't call or check in. He's gotten remarried and had another baby. I wouldn't be surprised if he doesn't admit to having an older son."

"I'm sorry," Sienna whispered automatically.

"Me, too, but mostly for my ex-husband. I never want my son to feel like it was his fault that his daddy didn't want to be a part of his life."

"Sometimes you can't help that. What would you do if Davey wanted to pursue a relationship with his dad or if your ex tried to come back into his life?"

Emily inclined her head, as if weighing the question in her mind. "I'd allow it to happen, but I'd be there to support Davey and what he needed along the way."

"My mom can't stand the fact that I'm here." Sienna reached out a hand, placed it on Emily's arm and squeezed. "Your son is going to turn out great." She gave a small laugh. "Unlike me. It's obvious you want what's best for him, and he has Jase, too."

"You're doing okay," Emily answered.

"Other than the fact that I've upended your and Jase's lives and quite possibly put my father in the hospital."

"Other than that," Emily agreed and pain speared through Sienna's chest. "I'm joking," Emily added quickly. "But things definitely took a turn toward more complicated today. Don't let that scare you off."

"Complicated has never been my favorite thing," Sienna admitted.

"Stick around long enough and you'll learn to appreciate it."

Jase appeared in the waiting room at that moment. Emily set aside the clipboard and rose from her seat to move forward, throwing her arms around his neck. They stood together for several long moments, holding on to each other tight.

Sienna glanced over and met Cole's dark gaze as he and Noah came to stand to one side of the couple. She could imagine holding on to him in that same way, and she felt a pang of envy that she might not get that chance.

"How is he?" she asked, rising from the chair.

"He's stable," Jase answered. He let go of Emily and moved toward Sienna. To her surprise, he leaned in for an awkward hug as relief filled her. "Thanks for getting help to him so quickly. The doctor says it might have saved his life."

Sienna felt her mouth drop open, unsure of what to say in response. "I thought you'd blame me." Immediately she knew that was the wrong response but couldn't retract it now.

Her brother only shook his head. "He's been on heart medicine for the past few years but isn't good about taking his pill every day."

He was giving her an out, but Sienna couldn't allow herself to take it. "I fought with him. He was angry and upset."

"You really must not remember much from our childhood," he said, one side of his mouth curving. "Arguing is Dad's love language. It would probably be easier if there was a bad guy in this situation, but we're just going to have to deal with things the hard way."

Emily peered around Jase's arm. "You could use a little work on accepting kindness," she told Sienna. "And not rushing off before dessert is served."

"I'll remember that for next time." Sienna returned Emily's smile, her heart swelling. The situation still wasn't perfect, but somehow it seemed like she might be able to forge a relationship with her estranged family after all.

"Can we see him?" Emily asked, taking Jase's hand in hers.

Jase shook his head. "He's resting now. The doctor expects him out of ICU by this afternoon. They think he'll only have to spend one night in the hospital, and we should be able to visit later today." He met Sienna's gaze again. "I'll call you when we know more"

She nodded, blinking back tears she didn't want anyone to see.

Cole stepped forward. "I'll give you a ride back to Declan's to pick up your car."

"I can take her," Jase said, shifting to block Cole from reaching for her.

"I've got it," Cole told him, confusion marring his movie-star features.

"I don't think so," Jase countered.

Sienna glanced at Emily and raised a brow.

"Okay, boys," the other woman said, moving between them. "Enough for now. Jase, we need to finish filling out paperwork and insurance forms. Cole, if you need to get back to work, I'm sure Noah can take Sienna."

"I'll take her," Cole repeated, his jaw clenched tight like he'd read something in Jase's expression that sat with him wrong.

"Text me later, Em," Noah said. He turned to Sienna and winked. "Welcome to having a big brother," he told her and walked away.

Emily put a hand on Jase's arm and pushed him toward the chairs where she'd left the clipboard. "We'll call you as soon as we know anything about your dad." Her tone was more chipper than Sienna had ever heard it.

"Let's go," Cole said and turned on his heel.

She stood where she was a moment longer, not sure

what she was missing in the exchange between the two long-time friends.

"Did Jase do something to make you mad?" she asked as she caught up to Cole's long strides.

"No."

"Did you have an argument?"

"Nope." Cole didn't glance her way but held open the door as she passed through.

She turned and reached out, placing both her hands on his arms. "What happened? You two are best friends."

"He's stepping into the role of protective older brother." He looked past her, his eyes unreadable.

Sienna felt color flood her cheeks. "I find that hard to believe. He doesn't even want me here."

"Don't let him fool you. Jase cares." He opened the Jeep's door and she got in, fatigue coursing through her now that the adrenaline had worn off. "Are you okay?"

She nodded. "I'll be fine, although waiting for an update is going to drive me crazy."

He dropped a quick kiss on her lips, then walked around the front of the SUV and climbed in the driver's side. "Have dinner with me later," he said, pulling away from the curb.

"I'm not sure—"

"We can change plans if you hear from Jase." An unspoken promise flickered in his gorgeous brown eyes, and she tried not to moan out loud. "Give it a chance, Sienna. Just one date."

"One date," she agreed, tamping down the delight and uncertainty that warred inside her, not to mention the hallelujah chorus her lower half was singing.

She could totally handle dinner with Cole, sure and steady and able to make butterflies dance across her chest with one smoldering glance. She could handle anything, she told herself, then sent up a silent prayer of thanks when no bolt of lightning appeared to strike her down for the lie.

Chapter Thirteen

"This is ridiculous," Sienna said. "The worst idea ever." She reached for the zipper on the back of the dress Paige had convinced her to wear to dinner with Cole.

"Don't you dare," Paige said, grabbing her arms and turning her until she faced the mirror. "That dress is amazing on you. Cole is going to lose his mind."

"That's not a good thing," Sienna said with a huff.

"It's great," Paige countered.

"How can I go out on a date with my father in the hospital? People will think I'm living up to my mom's awful reputation and only caring about myself."

"You have to eat dinner." Paige grabbed a bottle of perfume from the dresser in her room and spritzed Sienna. "You've talked to Jase twice since you got back here. He'll call you if anything changes with Declan's condition."

A loud hammering sounded from outside the bedroom window, and Paige made a face. "I hate construction," she said.

"How's it coming?"

"The contractor thinks he's got things under control, and I definitely appreciate that he's got the guys working late most nights to get the job done more quickly. But the water damage caused several floor joists to rot. Since the joists apparently hold up the actual floor, it's not good."

"Sounds expensive."

"Exactly," Paige agreed, then sighed. "And it's money I don't have. I'm going to have to call my mom and ask for a loan or tell her I'll be late on the mortgage payment for another month. I can't open for business without a floor and there's no money coming in without paying guests."

"I thought you were only going to share good news with your mom so she won't worry about you."

"That was the plan, but plans change. I'm not giving up on The Bumblebee. I just need to convince Mom not to give up on me."

"I hope she agrees."

"Yeah." Paige closed her eyes for a moment, then gave her head a little shake and opened them again. "But tonight is about you and our sexy sheriff. Do you think he carries handcuffs?"

"Only when I'm on duty."

Both women whirled around to find Cole standing at the bedroom door.

"I knocked," he said, holding up his hands, palms out, "but no one heard me over the hammering."

"You look quite handsome, Sheriff Bennett," Paige said with a wink. "Although the lack of handcuffs is a bit of a disappointment."

"We'll make do," Cole told her in his deep, rumbling voice.

Sienna was pretty sure she let out a whimper because Paige and Cole both turned to stare at her.

"It was my stomach growling," she lied, pressing a hand to her belly. "I'm hungry."

Paige grinned as she pushed Sienna toward Cole. "I just bet you are. Have a good night, you two. Be safe. Do lots of things I won't have a chance to."

"Thanks for letting me borrow the dress," Sienna said over her shoulder.

"Thank you *very* much," Cole echoed.

His whiskey-colored gaze burned into hers as he took her hand and lifted it, turning it over and placing a soft kiss on the inside of her wrist. "You're beautiful," he whispered and her knees felt like they were made of jelly.

"You, too," she blurted, then flashed a smile. "I mean, you look handsome tonight. Every night really. And during the day. But tonight especially, I guess."

"Maybe stop talking now," Paige called from behind her. Cole laughed and Sienna felt her cheeks go hot. What was it about this man that turned her into a babbling schoolgirl with her first crush?

He wore a pair of dark jeans and a crisp white button-down that made his tanned skin look even more golden. The sleeves were rolled up to the elbows, and the hair that peppered his forearms was somehow the sexiest thing she'd ever seen.

"I'm pathetic," she muttered, and Cole grabbed her hand and squeezed.

He waved to one of the workers, then led her out of the house. As soon as the front door had closed behind them, he turned and claimed her mouth, the kiss gentle and intense at the same time.

Her eyes drifted shut as she lost herself in the feel of him. This was what she wanted, to forget everything in her life except the way Cole's touch made her body come to life.

All too soon, he pulled away. "Thank you," he whispered, pressing his forehead to hers.

"For kissing you?"

"For agreeing to go out with me."

She should tell him it didn't mean anything. She needed to eat and wanted a distraction while she waited for news on her dad. But she couldn't make her mouth form the words, because it *did* mean something to her.

Yes, Cole was handsome as sin, but her connection to him was way more than a physical attraction. She loved his honesty and integrity, the way he tried to take care of her even when she didn't need him to. She liked the person she was when they were together. He made her feel more confident because he expected more from her than anyone ever had.

"I'm glad you asked," she told him, then fused her mouth to his. By the time she pulled back, they were both breathing heavily and Sienna felt like her whole body was on fire.

"But we should get dinner," she added, not trusting herself to share her bone-deep yearning to be close to him. Sienna had always stayed emotionally distant from the people around her. It was a defense mechanism, something to ensure she wouldn't be hurt.

Cole made her want to throw caution and all her self-preservation instincts to the wind and open herself up completely. It was terrifying and exhilarating at the same time, like climbing the first hill on a roller coaster when the car was cresting the top and about to careen down the other side.

"You're too practical for your own good," he said with

a low chuckle. "But let me ply you with food and spirits and then we'll see where this takes us."

"Romantic," she said, elbowing him as they walked to his truck.

"I have my moments," he told her with a wink.

"I just bet you do."

She climbed into the truck and fastened her seat belt, her insides still tingling from his kiss.

He pulled away from the curb, surprising her when he turned away from town.

"Where are we going?"

"It's a surprise."

She glanced at him out of the corner of her eye. "I hope this isn't some covert plan to dump me over the county line because I'm too much trouble."

He kept his eyes on the road in front of them. "Apparently I like trouble."

She tried—and failed—to hide her smile at his words.

A few minutes later, the truck's front dipped as he maneuvered onto a dirt road and drove over a deep rut. Sienna's stomach lurched in response.

She wasn't sure what to expect from this night. Her past dating experience had always been completely traditional and boring.

Dinner at a trendy restaurant, sometimes dancing at a nightclub or a round of tennis at the country club. After a few weeks, there would be the obligatory family get-together—usually Sunday brunch or happy hour with business colleagues. All of it on an appropriate timeline that showed interest—but not too much—and a sense of decorum that Sienna now recognized had been one of the things that had made her feel stifled and sick to death of her own life.

Everything with Cole felt new and exciting, and the unknown of it thrilled her.

"We're here," he said, pulling onto the narrow shoulder.

"Where's here?"

"Dinner," he answered. "Although with the way you look tonight, I'm second-guessing my plan."

"Do you have a plan?"

"You trust me, right?"

"Well, I trust that you're not a secret sheriff serial killer."

"Good to know," he said with a grin.

He got out of the truck and moved around to her side, opening the door for her. "We don't have to go far."

She nodded and stepped out, figuring she might as well be game for whatever adventure he had planned. At least it was taking her mind off her father and his condition.

She silently congratulated herself for choosing a pair of comfortable wedge heels from Paige's closet so she wasn't worried about breaking an ankle on the trail.

Cole took a cooler out of the truck's cargo bed and started up the path peeking out from the heavily wooded area.

They'd only walked about twenty-five feet when the forest opened into a picturesque meadow, complete with a view of the mountains and a rustic picnic table set up in the middle of the field.

She stepped into the clearing, then spun around in a slow circle, marveling at the quiet beauty around them. "Is there some manual they gave you when you moved here about hidden vistas in Crimson?"

He flashed a wide smile. "I talk to a lot of people in my line of work. I ask questions. Privacy is important to me, but I don't want to miss out on how great this area is because of it. I'll take the road or the picnic area less traveled when I can."

"I'm overdressed."

"You look perfect."

"It looks like the picnic table is already set."

He nodded, looking almost sheepish. "I came out earlier and got things ready."

She followed him to the center of the meadow. A linen covered the picnic table, which was set for two. "I hope you're not disappointed that we're not at a restaurant in town. It seemed like you might get a bunch of questions about your dad. I thought you could use a break, and we're closer to the hospital here than if we'd gone downtown."

"So you cooked?"

He placed the cooler on one of the long benches. "Not exactly," he told her, opening the lid. "But I'm great at ordering carryout." He took out several cardboard food containers. "There's a new Italian place on the way to Aspen. Best manicotti ever."

He placed the boxes on the table, then pulled out a bottle of wine and two glasses.

"You went to so much trouble," she murmured.

"We can hit the town next time if you want," he told her with a boyish smile that melted her heart.

"This is perfect." She leaned in to brush a kiss across his jaw. What she wanted to say was that Cole was perfect. Perfect for her. But she was afraid to reveal too much, terrified at how serious her feelings for him had become in such a short time.

He uncorked the wine and she held the glasses while he poured. They toasted to Declan's health and new beginnings, then Cole opened the containers and served them both crisp green salad and a scrumptious-smelling portion of pasta.

"It's amazing," she said after taking a bite, the combination of tangy sauce and rich cheese making her want to moan with pleasure.

"What's your favorite restaurant in Chicago?" he asked.

She smiled. "The shawarma food truck that parks around the corner from my condo. I'm not much of a cook either. I eat there at least twice a week."

"Do you miss the city?"

She forked up another bite but paused before putting it in her mouth. "Not really, which is strange. Everything in my regular life was so structured. I thought that's how I liked it, but now I see that it was also suffocating me."

"Structure isn't a bad thing," he said, taking a sip of wine.

She smiled. "So says the lawman with the military background. I wish I'd questioned things more when I was growing up, and even as an adult. My mom made it clear that I should be grateful for the life we had, and I was. But I didn't choose it. I never learned to figure out what I wanted. You'd think with the Crenshaw blood in me I would have rebelled or gone off the rails or something. Instead I was just a dutiful little sheep following the flock."

She put down her fork and picked up the wineglass. "I'm mostly disappointed in myself at this point for letting other people decide how I should live my life."

"You can always change that."

"What about you?" she asked, twirling the stem of the wineglass between her fingers.

"What about me?"

"Is there something you'd change about your—?"

"Nope. My life is just fine."

"What about your brother? Aren't you curious about where he is now? He's the only family you have, right?"

Cole's jaw clenched, but he nodded.

"You could reach out to him. Try to mend the rift—"

"I told you I don't even know if he's still alive."

"You're twins," she insisted. "I have to believe you'd know if something awful had happened."

"Yeah," he agreed reluctantly, running a hand over his jaw. "I'd know. But Shep made his choice after Dad died. The fact that he didn't come back for Mom's funeral... I can't forgive that."

"You could at least try to contact him."

"I have no idea where he is at this point."

"People have to work hard to hide in this day and age. One quick Google search and I bet—"

"I don't need him," Cole snapped. "I don't need anyone. My life is fine the way it is."

She forced herself to swallow the bite of pasta she'd just taken, even though it felt like it had turned to sawdust in her mouth. "Good to know."

Cole blew out a breath. "I didn't mean that the way it sounded."

"It's fine," she lied.

"Sienna, I'm—"

He broke off when both of their phones chirped wildly. Sienna grabbed hers from her purse as Cole pulled his from his back pocket.

"He's awake," she whispered, knowing that Cole would understand she was talking about her father. Jase had texted them both.

She let out a shuddery breath and pressed her fingers to her mouth when a sob threatened to emerge. Cole immediately stood and came around to her side of the table. He dropped down next to her and wrapped a hand around her shoulder.

She buried her face in the crook of his neck, breathing in the strong, safe scent of him. He rubbed his open palm in wide circles on her back, murmuring soothing words against her ear.

"I'll take you to the hospital," he told her.

"We haven't finished dinner," she argued weakly. "Jase is there and—"

"It's okay," he promised. "We can take a rain check on dessert. You need to be with your family right now."

Family. It was still difficult to believe that just by coming to Crimson and inserting herself in their lives that Declan and Jase were her family. Not after so many years of absence from her life.

But that's how it felt. They were family. The bond between the three of them was fragile, but it tied them together nonetheless.

"Thank you for understanding," she said as he gathered their plates and leftover food.

They made quick work of putting away the picnic, then returned down the trail to the truck. They were only ten minutes to the hospital, but the drive seemed interminable to Sienna. She vacillated between guilt that she hadn't been there when Declan first woke to regret that she'd effectively ruined the perfect date Cole had planned. Once again, nothing she did was quite right.

"Do you want me to go in with you?" Cole asked, parking in front of the hospital's entrance.

"I should go on my own," she told him, then leaned across the console to give him a quick kiss. "Thank you again. Tonight was the best date I've ever had."

He traced a finger along her jaw. "And the shortest, I'm guessing."

"Rain check," she promised, giving him one last kiss before hurrying into the hospital.

Chapter Fourteen

The swoosh of the elevator doors sounded particularly loud as Sienna exited. She checked in with the nurse at the charge desk, then walked down the hall toward her father's room.

She knocked softly and, with a deep breath, pushed open the door. Jase immediately straightened from a chair to one side of the bed, rubbing a hand over his eyes as he moved toward her.

"Sorry I wasn't here earlier." Her gaze tracked to Declan, lying in the hospital bed with his eyes closed and a sheet pulled up to just below his chest. He looked peaceful. Silver whiskers shadowed his jaw and a long tube peeked out from the gap in the front of the hospital gown, attached to a heart monitor next to the bed.

"Don't worry about it," he answered. "He only woke up for a few minutes, then drifted back to sleep."

"Is that good or bad?"

"The doctors believe he'll make a full recovery. They did an angioplasty for a blockage in one of his arteries and inserted a stent to keep it open long-term. He's going to need to finally take his diet more seriously, and we'll need to make sure he starts exercising regularly. But if we can convince him to give up the junk food and make his health a priority, he should be around to be a pain in the butt for a good while."

She laughed softly. "Cheese puffs," she murmured. "I remember him loving cheese puffs. He'd deny it, but his fingertips were always stained orange."

"Still loves them," Jase confirmed. He took a step back and looked her up and down. "You look nice."

She smoothed a self-conscious hand over the front of her dress. "I borrowed it from Paige. I had… I went out… I was having dinner when you texted."

"With Paige?" he asked, one thick brow lifting.

She shook her head but didn't give any more information.

"Then it must have been Cole." His tone was low and fairly disapproving.

"He's your best friend," she pointed out. "Is there some problem with me having dinner with him?"

"You're my sister," he answered, as if that explained everything.

It was odd but sweet to hear him refer to her in that way, sounding both overprotective and exasperated. It was clear Jase couldn't explain how they'd gotten to this place any more than she could.

She raised a brow. "From what I heard, not that long ago you wanted Cole close to me so he could make sure I didn't have any evil plans for my time in Crimson."

One side of his mouth curved. "Evil isn't quite the right term. Things changed. I'm not trying to chase you away, Sienna, and Cole is a friend. But he's not a long-term bet for a woman."

"Who says I'm interested in that?"

"No one." He shook his head. "But I hope you're in our lives for the long term. It's taken too many years to get to this point, and I don't want anyone to mess that up. Dad can handle that all on his own."

"I'm stuck in this damn bed," a gravelly voice said, "and you're going to diss me."

"When did you start using the word *diss*?" Jase asked as they both turned to the bed, where Declan had propped himself up against the pillow.

"My neighbor has a twelve-year-old boy. He downloaded Urban Dictionary on that fancy phone you got me."

"Lord help us," Jase muttered.

Sienna moved to the side of the bed. "How are you feeling, Dad?"

Declan stared at her for a moment. "You called me Dad," he said, adjusting the sheet. "I should come close to dying more often."

"Don't even think about it," she countered.

"I'm fine, baby girl." He lifted one thin shoulder, then let it drop. "It takes more than a wee clogged artery to finish me off."

"I'm glad." She reached out and squeezed his hand. "You gave me quite a scare."

"Let's be clear." Declan looked between the two of them. "This episode had nothing to do with Sienna. It was me and the fact that I can barely remember to put the toilet seat down, let alone take my heart medication every day."

"I know," Jase told him, affection clear in his tone. "You were lucky Sienna was with you when it happened."

"True dat," Declan said, nodding.

Sienna stifled a laugh and glanced at Jase.

"Overmedicated," he said in a stage whisper.

Declan laughed. "No such thing."

Sienna felt a strange sense of happiness bubble up in her chest. It was surreal to be here with her dad and brother, a family gathered when someone needed help, making light of a situation that had clearly scared all of them.

"How do you feel?" She let go of his hand and moved the chair closer to the bed.

"Like a herd of cattle trampled over my chest." He shrugged. "Pretty normal."

"You shouldn't make light of it. Jase said they've talked to you about diet and exercise. You need to comply with the doctor's orders."

Declan looked past her to Jase. "Did you pay her to say all that?"

"She cares," Jase answered, "even though you probably don't deserve it."

"I definitely don't," her father agreed.

"I care," Sienna murmured, still surprised to find it was true. Not just because she felt guilty that she'd been arguing with her father when he collapsed. She wanted him to be well. She wanted a chance at some kind of relationship with both of these men. The feeling of abandonment that had been her companion for so long was slowly fading, replaced by the bright glow of her newly forged connection.

Her father met her gaze for a long moment, his blue eyes tired but tender as he seemed to drink her in.

"You two should go," he said gruffly. "You've seen that I'm gonna make it. Go home and get some rest."

"I'll stay for a bit," Sienna said immediately. "Jase can go. He's been here all day."

Jase rubbed a hand over his whiskered jaw. "Are you sure? I can—"

"Your sister will stay," Declan said, and Jase gave a small smile, seeming pleased by his father's use of the word *sister*.

Sienna was secretly pleased, as well. She appreciated this unfamiliar sense of belonging.

Jase gave her a short, somewhat less awkward hug than before, then squeezed his father's shoulder. "Rest," he said. "You've got a new granddaughter to meet in a few weeks, so you'll need plenty of energy."

"I promise," Declan answered, and Jase left the room.

"You want to talk more about all the things I did wrong?" her dad asked when they were alone.

"Of course not. You're in a hospital bed."

He raised a brow. "It's the perfect location. I can't leave and they've got paddles all over this place if things go south."

"That's morbid."

"And a joke."

"At least I know I didn't get my sense of humor from you." She adjusted her dress, then picked an invisible piece of lint from the fabric. "Thanks for not dying."

"Your sense of humor has hope after all." He waved a finger at her. "Why are you all dolled up tonight?"

"I was out to dinner when Jase texted to say you'd woken."

"With Cole Bennett?"

She shrugged. "I had to eat."

Declan tipped back his head and laughed. "Well played, baby girl. Not that I have any business doling out parental advice, but be careful with Cole. I have enough demons that I've gotten damn good at recognizing them in others. Our sheriff is a stand-up kind of guy, but he's got some of his own stuff to work through. I don't want you getting hurt."

"That sounded suspiciously like parental advice." She adjusted her position on the chair, settled in to the cushions. "I doubt anyone can top the issues I'm dealing with on my own."

Declan shook his head. "You're not like Cole. But you do what you need to. Jase and I are here now, and we'll catch you if you fall."

She swallowed against the emotion rising in her chest. Yes, she'd grown up with a mom and stepdad. She'd never been alone, but somehow she'd felt it all her life. The idea that there were now people in her corner made her heart sing.

Declan leaned back against the pillow, and she watched as his eyes drifted closed. Pretty soon he was softly snoring. She closed her eyes, feeling a greater sense of peace than she had in years.

It was still dark when Cole opened his front door, revealing Sienna standing on the porch.

"Did I wake you?" she asked, the corners of her mouth pulling down. She still wore the gorgeous dress from the night before, the fabric wrinkled in places. Her long hair was pulled back in a messy bun, and there were smudges under her eyes that looked like they'd come from lack of sleep. She remained the most beautiful woman he'd ever laid eyes on.

"It's ten minutes to five," he answered, stifling a yawn. He'd thrown on an old T-shirt and a pair of basketball shorts on the way to the door. "Even the birds aren't awake yet."

"Sorry," she murmured, taking a step back. "I'll go so you can—"

"Not so fast." He grabbed her arm and pulled her closer, lifting her over the threshold and swinging the door shut with his foot. "I'm awake now and damn glad to see you." Pressing a kiss to the top of her head, he breathed in the scent of her, his body revving to life in an instant. "Tell me about your dad."

"He's fine. I spent the night at the hospital."

"Big step."

"It felt right. He and Jase and I had…" she shrugged, as if not sure what words to choose "…a moment last night. It was like we were a family."

"You *are* family," he reminded her.

"But for the first time, I felt it."

"Good for you, Sienna."

"When I left the hospital, this was the only place I wanted to go."

"Good for me," he whispered.

She ducked her head, smoothed a loose strand of hair away from her face. "Any chance you've still got the brownies I spied earlier at the bottom of the cooler?"

He chuckled. "Now I understand why you're here. I'm playing second-string to Katie's brownies."

"Only a little," she admitted.

They walked to his kitchen and he handed her the box of brownies while he took a gallon of milk from the fridge. "Unless you want me to make coffee?"

"Milk is fine."

She lowered herself to one of the chairs at his kitchen table. His breath caught as he watched her in the simple task of unwrapping the sweet treat. Cole had been living alone for a lot of years, and he liked it that way. He was a solitary person by nature, but Sienna looked like she belonged in his house. She made it feel like a home, something Cole hadn't allowed himself to have in a long time.

He brought the milk and two glasses to the table and pulled out the chair next to her. She took a small bite of the brownie, her pink tongue darting out to catch a crumb that clung to her bottom lip.

She didn't say anything more about her dad, and Cole didn't ask, content to share these quiet minutes with her.

Content wasn't a word he normally associated with himself, but he was smart enough to appreciate the new sensation.

And when Sienna stood and took a step forward, so close the front of her legs brushed the inside of his thighs, he stayed perfectly still, not wanting to do anything to screw up the moment.

She bent forward and kissed him, tasting of chocolate, and right now Cole was the biggest sugar addict on the planet.

"Can we finish the rest of last night now?" she asked against his mouth. "Or do you have to get ready for work?"

"I'll make time for you whenever you want." He straightened, scooping her into his arms as he did. She felt right there, and his heart sang as she settled in against his chest.

His house was simple, a two-bedroom bungalow that hadn't been updated since the mid-seventies. He didn't care about much other than a clean set of sheets, a stocked fridge and a big-screen television. For a second, he wondered what Sienna thought of it. Clearly, she'd grown up in an affluent community in Chicago, and he guessed most of her previous boyfriends had fast cars and fancy houses.

"I love it here," she whispered, as if she could read his mind. "There's no place I'd rather be."

He walked into his bedroom and set her down, cupping her cheeks between his palms. "I don't deserve you," he said, then inwardly cringed. Why the hell did he have to go and admit something like that?

Her eyes clouded, then she gave a small shake of her head. "You're a good man, Cole. Don't try to deny it."

Now that he'd said the words, he couldn't back down from them. "Jase was smart to warn you off of me. I don't want to hurt you."

"You won't."

The unwavering confidence in her tone did funny things to his insides, loosening parts of him that had been tightly caged for so long. The sensation was both exhilarating and disturbing, like he was a toy top spinning out of control. He held on to Sienna to ground him.

He breathed her in, then kissed her until his doubts had returned to the shadowed recesses where they lurked. She pressed closer, moaning softly when his palm grazed the underside of her breast.

"You're sure this is what you want?"

She took a few steps away, reaching her hands behind her back. The soft whir of a zipper being undone filled the quiet room. "Can I ask you a question?"

He sucked in a breath and nodded as the fabric of her dress dipped below her shoulders.

"Do you really think I came here for a brownie?" She wiggled a little and the dress pooled at her feet. She wore a black lace bra with matching panties and his knees threatened to give out. He already knew her body was perfection, but somehow this felt different. She was choosing him. Claiming him for her own.

He loved every second of it. Loved everything about this woman, not just her body but who she was on the inside—who he was when they were together. He paused as the implication of the emotions tumbling through him hit home. He couldn't *love* Sienna. He wouldn't let himself fall in love. Cole had seen how love could ruin a person. It had destroyed his mother, and he'd never make himself or anyone else that vulnerable.

He forced the breath in and out of his lungs, willing himself to stay in the present moment. Here with Sienna.

"Should I give you a hint as to the answer?" Color flooded her cheeks as she pulled out the elastic that held back her hair. Blond waves fell over her shoulders, and she tugged on her lower lip.

"I seriously do not deserve you," he whispered, "but I'm damn glad I've got you right now."

One side of her mouth kicked up. "So what are you going to do with me?"

"Everything," he answered as he shucked out of his shirt. He reached for her, and they fell to the bed together in a tangle of limbs. He nipped on her earlobe, and she skimmed her fingernails along his back.

He stood for a moment, pushing his boxers and shorts down over his hips.

"You're still wearing too much," he told her, arching a brow.

She lifted her back off the bed and unclasped her bra, letting the straps ease down her shoulders the same way the dress had earlier. This impromptu striptease was even sexier, and he reminded himself he was a lucky man to have this woman in his bed. In his life.

She reached for her panties, but he moved forward and brushed her fingers out of the way. "Allow me."

He tugged them over her hips, then pushed apart her legs, taking in the heavenly view he had of her body from this vantage point.

His hands moved along her thighs until he reached her center, and he almost lost himself when she arched off the bed, moaning as he touched her.

"Cole," she said, her voice hoarse, "I don't think—"

"That's right," he interrupted, "no thinking right now."

He couldn't resist following his fingers with his mouth and was rewarded with a soft cry and the word "Yes."

She continued to make the most beautiful little noises, finally crying out as he felt a tremor snake through her body. He reached into the nightstand drawer for a condom, then entered her in one swift thrust, unable to hold back any longer.

Sienna wrapped her arms around his neck, and they moved together, pressure building in Cole as she whispered his name. Pleasure burst over him like a shower of stars, brilliant and bright, and Cole never wanted the moment to end.

Chapter Fifteen

"Where are you rushing off to?"

Sienna gave a weak smile as she fastened her bra, then reached for her dress, which was still in a crumpled pile on the floor next to the bed. It was remarkably difficult to get dressed while keeping the sheet around her body.

"I need to go home." She cleared her throat. "To the inn. I'm sure you need to get to work and…" She stretched out a toe, trying to inch the dress closer. "I should call the office. I've been missing a lot of client meetings so I check in with my assistant first thing in the morning. It makes me feel like I'm not totally out of touch."

Cole had been in the bathroom for a few minutes, which had given her much needed time to collect herself after the best two orgasms of her life. She'd never thought herself the kind of woman to be affected by great sex, although maybe that was because up until Cole, she'd only had mediocre intimate relationships. Mediocre at best, as the saying went.

"You're talking fast like you're uncomfortable," Cole said, bending forward and plucking her dress off the floor.

She sighed and reached out a hand. "Babbling," she muttered. "It's called babbling."

One corner of his mouth kicked up, then he dropped down next to her on the bed. He'd put on his boxers, although his bare chest was plenty distracting. She was currently dealing with something way more serious than physical attraction. She was falling hard and fast for Sheriff Cole Bennett.

Falling in love.

It was ridiculous and painfully ill-advised. Cole had all but admitted he was going to hurt her. Her brother had warned her. Her father had warned her.

Sienna might be new to having so many men who cared in her life, yet she wasn't a fool. She'd be an idiot to let herself fall in love with Cole, not when her time in Crimson might be temporary and he hadn't given her any sign he wanted anything long-term.

"I'm an idiot," she muttered, quickly ripping off the sheet and pulling up her dress. It had been easy to feel confident about her body when she was in the throes of passion. Now she felt too exposed.

"I like the babbling," Cole said, giving her arm a playful nudge.

She stood, turning away from him, and slipped her arms into the dress, struggling to tug the zipper all the way up. She felt his warm body at her back a moment later. With gentle fingers, he gathered her hair and draped it over one shoulder, then zipped up the dress.

"I know it's silly," she protested, "that I get nervous around you." She grabbed her shoes off the floor and forced herself to meet his gaze. "I'm sorry I'm bad at the morning-after stuff."

"Technically, it's still the morning of."

She groaned. Why couldn't she manage to act normal five minutes after the best sex of her life? "Even worse."

"You're cute." He dropped a kiss on the tip of her nose.

She wanted to splay her hands across his bare chest, push him back down on the bed and have her merry way with him.

"I *really* need to go," she said instead.

"Okay." He traced the tip of one finger along her jaw. "But promise me you won't let this freak you out. It's not a big deal."

If they gave out Academy Awards for keeping a poker face, Sienna would be a front-runner. It felt like Cole had just driven his fist into her chest. She could actually feel her heart shriveling as his words spread like a cancer through her.

"Of course," she agreed, forcing a bright smile. He frowned, as if he detected the hysterical edge to her voice but couldn't quite figure out what had caused it. "I'll catch you on the flip side, Sheriff." She placed a quick kiss on his mouth, then turned and gave what she hoped was a jaunty wave.

"I'll check in at the hospital later," he called, and she lifted her arm again, then pulled it tight to her side when she realized her fingers were shaking like an aspen leaf in the wind.

She grabbed her purse and quickly let herself out of Cole's house, only realizing as she stood on the front porch that she had no mode of transportation to get home. Not home. To the inn. She had no home at the moment.

Tears of pain and embarrassment pricked at the backs of Sienna's eyes. Afraid Cole would realize she'd taken an Uber from the hospital to his house, she hurried down the sidewalk and around the corner. Still somewhat unfamiliar with Crimson's geography, despite the small-town flavor, she punched the B&B's address into the GPS on her phone and began walking the neighborhood streets in the direction it sent her.

The morning was lovely, as seemed to be the norm in Colorado. A chill hung in the air but the sun shining from a clear blue sky was quickly warming things. She held her heels in one hand, appreciating the feel of the sidewalk beneath her feet. The cool pavement acted to ground her, helping her to remember she was more than just her aching heart.

She waved to an older woman sweeping off her front walk. The woman stared for several seconds, then called, "Dana?"

"I'm her daughter," Sienna answered, slowing her pace.

The woman walked closer. "Of course. I heard you were in town. You really do look so much like her."

"I've been told that most of my life. Were you friends with my mother?" She suddenly had an urge to know more about her mom's time in Crimson. How did things get so far off track and why did Dana feel like she had no choice but to leave the way she did?

"Lordy, no." The woman gave a dismissive laugh. "She and Declan hung with a wild crowd. Always up to no good. It's a wonder you and your brother survived it."

"Oh." Not that Sienna necessarily denied the truth of the woman's words but that didn't make them any easier to hear.

"Those two were the most irresponsible, reckless—"

"Well, nice talking to you," Sienna interrupted. She couldn't stand to hear any more.

"Someone told me you were different," the woman continued, scrunching up her nose like she'd smelled something rotten. "More like your brother." Her gaze raked over Sienna, disapproval clear in her dull brown eyes. "But I doubt you put on that outfit this morning. It's clear the Crenshaw blood runs strong in you, missy."

Paige had joked about the walk of shame the first time Sienna spent the night at Cole's, but this woman wasn't making a joke.

"I take that as a compliment," Sienna said, despite the embarrassment washing over her. She had nothing to feel guilty about—spending the night in an uncomfortable hospital chair didn't constitute wild and reckless. She lifted her chin and adopted the haughty glare she'd watched her mother perfect over the years. "Have a lovely morning," she said in a clipped tone, then walked away without a backward glance.

It was another half mile to The Bumblebee, and Sienna walked it quickly, her gaze focused on the sidewalk in front of her. She passed several morning joggers but didn't bother greeting any of them. The woman's words had hit their mark. Was that the sort of judgment her mom had received from this small community? It left a sour taste in Sienna's mouth.

The front door of the inn was open and she called out a greeting to Paige as she entered the foyer. The sound of hammering had already started, and she hoped for her friend's sake the construction project would finish soon.

"Sienna, you're back." Paige rushed from the direction of the kitchen, curls bouncing.

"No 'walk of shame' comments," Sienna said with a dry laugh. "I've had enough—"

"I have another guest," Paige blurted. "She arrived this morning and insisted on taking the room across from yours. I told her she'd be more comfortable at one of the hotels in town, but—"

"Where have you been and why are you dressed like that?"

Sienna sucked in a breath, dropping the shoes she'd been holding to the wood floor with a thud. "Oh, no," she whispered under her breath.

"Oh, yes," Paige answered in a similar whisper.

"Mom, what are you doing here?"

Dana Pierce came down the steps as if she was being presented at a debutante ball, shoulders straight, chin lifted, two fingers gingerly skimming the wooden handrail. As if Sienna's mother needed support. Her blond hair was pulled back into a neat chignon, putting her elegant throat and the strand of pearls around her neck on full display. She wore an outfit Sienna had come to think of as her mother's uniform—slim trousers and a crisp button-down shirt, slightly fitted, with the collar starched so that it stood stiff like a soldier at boot camp.

Today's shirt was a shade of pale green, perhaps as a nod to the pine forests that surrounded Crimson. Matching the occasion was sort of a thing for Dana. Pink for Valentine's Day, yellow on Easter and a pattern of red and white stripes around the holidays. Festive but understated.

"You haven't called in several days," Dana said, as if that explained everything.

"So you flew to Colorado?" Sienna pressed a hand to her forehead.

"Coffee?" Paige asked.

Sienna nodded. "Yes, please."

"Mrs. Pierce?"

"Half a cup with a tablespoon of creamer." Dana pierced Paige with one of her laser-beam glares as she came to stand at the bottom of the stairs. "No more than a tablespoon."

"I'll measure," Paige offered quickly, then hurried toward the kitchen.

"You could have just asked for light creamer," Sienna said with an eye roll.

"How do I know what that woman considers light?" Dana swept an arm toward the front room, which was crowded with the furniture and knickknacks Paige had moved so the guys could work on the floor. "I appreciate details, and it doesn't seem like the innkeeper cares much for them. How does one expect to run a business like this?"

"The floor had water damage. She's having it repaired. Paige has done a great job refurbishing this place, and she's a fantastic cook and generous hostess. The Bumblebee will succeed." Sienna wasn't sure why she felt the need to defend Paige, but it was easier than talking about her mother's unexpected appearance.

Dana sniffed. "I didn't rearrange my schedule to come here and talk about a ramshackle bed-and-breakfast."

Sienna inclined her head to study her mother, thinking about her encounter with the woman on her way home from Cole's. "What happened to you in Crimson?"

"I don't know what you mean. I arrived this morning and—"

"When I was a kid," Sienna clarified. "I've talked to several people who remember you and—"

"I changed."

"That could be the understatement of the century. Going from brunette to redhead or having bangs cut is a change. You left Crimson a party girl and made yourself into some sort of Grace Kelly or Jackie O. wannabee."

"That's ridiculous. I never wanted to be anyone but myself."

"Who are you *really*?" Sienna stepped closer, and her mother looked away.

"I'm a woman who fell in love with the wrong man and wanted to take my children away from the mess of our lives."

"You walked away so easily. You never drink and your idea of a party is a string quartet and cucumber sandwiches."

"This is who I am."

"But not who you were. I didn't realize the reputation you had here. I thought it was Dad."

Her mother's mouth pressed into a thin line. "Declan Crenshaw is your father by biology only. Do not call him *Dad* to me." She practically spit the word. "It's disrespectful to your stepfather, who's taken care of you all these years."

"Financially," Sienna muttered.

"Excuse me?"

"Craig Pierce has taken care of me financially, and I'm grateful to him. I always will be. But neither of us should pretend he has any real affection for me. He wanted you, and I was part of the package."

"That's not..." Her mother broke off because it was the truth and they both knew it. "Declan doesn't care about you either."

"He does," Sienna argued. "Jase, too. I was just never allowed to believe it."

"You don't know everything, Sienna."

"Because you'd never tell me anything. Dad has talked to me plenty, and he's apologized for the mistakes he made."

Dana let out a derisive laugh. "He hasn't told you the truth then."

Sienna threw up her hands. "Are you going to enlighten me?"

"I'm here to take you home." Her mother clasped her hands together in front of her chest. "We had dinner with Kevin the other night. He told us you'd moved your things out of the condo."

"I had Jennie do it. She's keeping them in her parents' garage until I get back."

"It was a hasty decision. Kevin wants another chance."

"He cheated on me," Sienna shouted. "Then blamed me for not being able to keep his junk in his pants."

"Don't be crude."

"You know what I discovered? It's not me. I'm not frigid. In fact, I had the best sex of my life just this morning and a big, fat..." She made the shape of an O with her fingers. "I had no complaints about my part in things."

"Sienna."

"It wasn't my fault," she yelled, then pressed a hand to her mouth. The hammering from the other room had stopped. Color flooded her cheeks as she imagined the workers listening to her outburst.

Paige breezed into the room, smiling widely but looking about as uncomfortable as Sienna felt at the moment. "Who's ready for coffee?" she asked brightly. "One tablespoon of creamer." She held out a mug to Sienna's mother. "Not a drop more."

Dana didn't take the mug. "I'm going to return to my room and gather my things," she said, her lips barely moving. "Paige, I believe you were correct in your assessment that I'd be better suited to a hotel in town. Sienna, we'll talk when you've calmed down. This behavior is unbecoming and not like you. Crimson has a bad effect on the women in our family. We leave for Denver the day after tomorrow. I'll have my travel agent make the flight arrangements."

Sienna clenched her hands into fists, focusing on

drawing air in and out of her lungs. The hammering re-
sumed, and her mother turned and walked up the stairs.

"Okay then," Paige said cheerily, moving into Sienna's
line of sight. "I think that went well."

Chapter Sixteen

The following morning, Cole sped along the winding road that led to Crimson's abandoned ski resort, the Jeep's lights flashing but its sirens silent. He was checking on a call the station had received that shots were being fired on the ski mountain.

It wasn't anywhere near ski season, not to mention no one in town had rights to be on that land anyway. Cole couldn't imagine the resort's new owner would want to hear about some crazy person popping off multiple rounds on private land.

Since the road was all but deserted this time of day, Cole kept the Jeep's siren off. If someone was trespassing or worse on resort property, he didn't want to warn them of his approach.

He parked in the lot, empty except for a gleaming black Porsche SUV near the far end. As he approached the vehicle, the distant sound of music wafted toward him. He shined his flashlight into the tinted windows, but the Porsche was empty.

He followed the sound of music—and more specifically *The Piña Colada Song*—up the stairs that led to the lodge's wraparound patio.

The ski resort had closed in the early nineties due to a bankruptcy filing and family disputes by the long-time owners. Some of the older deputies had shared that it used to be a popular spot for local teens right after it was abandoned, but that had changed in the ensuing years. Nowadays, he had someone check the property on a routine basis but not many people ventured out this way other than hikers or tourists who'd taken a wrong turn.

Beer cans lined the patio's wide rail, and Cole automatically put a hand on his weapon as he came around the corner.

A pair of long legs and expensive-looking sneakers came into view, and the next moment Cole let out a string of curses so vile it would have made his old army buddies blush. The man lounging in the chair was so similar to Cole in his features and build, it was almost like looking in a mirror. A mirror he wanted to punch with every fiber of his being.

"Hey, bro. I was wondering when you'd get here." Shep Bennett made a show of checking his watch, sun reflecting off the shiny face. "Twenty-four minutes from when I fired my first round. Not great response time, if you ask me." He hit a button on his phone to turn off the music, then picked up a .22 handgun from the arm of the weathered lounge chair where he was sitting and aimed at the beer cans.

"Don't you dare—"

Shep fired three shots and a trio of cans disappeared over the railing.

"Put it down and explain what the hell you're doing here."

Shep laughed as he placed the gun on the chair's arm again. "I'm letting off a little steam is all. You remember fun, don't you?"

Anger flooded through Cole, engulfing the relief he felt at seeing Shep safe after all these years. He grabbed the gun, unloaded the magazine and took the bullet out of the chamber. He stepped directly in front of his brother, blocking his view of the ski mountain. "Why does your idea of fun always involve being an idiot?"

Shep stood, walked to the patio's railing. "Guess I take after dad," he said and flicked the remaining beer can over the edge.

"You're going to clean all those up." Cole moved forward to stand next to his brother. "Then you can drive away from here—back to wherever life has taken you."

"That's a funny story," Shep muttered.

"Tell me you didn't steal the Porsche."

Shep turned, leaning a hip on the rail. "Give me a break, Cole. It's mine."

"Since when do you have that kind of money?"

"A lot can happen in seven years."

"Like Mom's funeral," Cole shot back. He saw pain flare in his brother's features before the smirk he remembered so well returned.

"You had to go there."

It wasn't just that Cole saw he'd upset Shep. He felt his brother's emotional pain, courtesy of the unexplainable connection he had with his twin. Shep might pretend he didn't care, but the truth was far more complicated.

"Where were you?" Cole asked.

Shep shrugged. "Arizona for a while. A few months in Mazatlán. Mainly I've been in California. The weather is—"

"February 12," Cole interrupted. "That was the day

I buried her. By myself. It would have killed her how little you care."

"The heart attack beat me to it," Shep ground out between clenched teeth. "You know I loved her. She knew it. I was down in Mexico when she died and couldn't get back in time."

"You never even called."

"To say what?" Shep crossed his arms over his chest. "What did you want from me? Were we supposed to commiserate over our shared loss? As if being orphaned was going to bring us suddenly closer. Dad ruined all of our lives."

"She died of a broken heart," Cole murmured.

"There was nothing I could have done about it at the time."

"You could have helped me deal with things."

Shep barked out a harsh laugh. "Give me a break. You've never needed a moment's help in your whole life. The stronger twin. The alpha. That's what Mom always called you."

"Only so she'd have an excuse to baby you."

"Baby me? That's rich."

Cole pushed away from the railing and paced along the edge of the patio. Shep exasperated him, but Cole didn't want this kind of animosity. It did neither of them any good to fight. Cole prided himself on keeping his temper in check and blamed the shock of seeing his brother after so long on his behavior.

His first instinct, after wanting to berate Shep for the business with the gun and beer cans, had been to rush forward and throw his arms around his twin. It felt like he'd stumbled upon an appendage he hadn't realized he'd been missing. A part of him had come home.

But Crimson wasn't Shep's home, and the fact that he'd

shown up without warning, clearly ready to antagonize Cole, didn't bode well for a brotherly reunion. Still, Cole felt like he had to try.

"It's good to see you despite everything."

"Liar." Shep flashed a small smile. "You always were a horrible liar. Half the time that's how Mom could tell us apart when we got into trouble."

"You were an expert," Cole agreed. "Yet somehow we both got into the same amount of trouble. Out with it, Shep. What are you doing here?" He held out his hands. "Why the big production to get me to this place? A phone call or a text would have worked fine."

"I figured it was time I visit my new home." Shep flashed a far too innocent smile. "Do you want to be the first person to welcome me to Crimson, Sheriff Bennett?"

Cole swallowed, feeling like he'd just downed a handful of sawdust. He and Shep were like oil and water, and Cole had made Crimson his own. It was one thing for his brother to pay an unexpected visit, but the thought that Shep might be in Colorado permanently was too much.

"Don't mess with me." He removed his sunglasses, made a show of cleaning them on his shirtfront. Trying to look casual. Trying to appear as if he wasn't losing his mind. "Crimson isn't your kind of place."

The town was Cole's place. He and his brother had never been good at sharing. Whether toys or friends or later women, if one twin claimed something or someone, there was an unspoken rule that the other let it go.

"I'm ready for a change." Shep lifted his arms and spun in a slow circle. "A new challenge."

"A development company bought the resort," Cole argued. "Even abandoned and in disrepair, the land is worth millions. Unless you've been running drugs for the past few years, there's no way you could do this on your own." He cursed, then added, "I sure as hell hope you're not running drugs."

"Dude, you've been binge-watching too many shows," Shep said, looking both amused and offended. "I'm the head of Trinity Development Company. Right after Dad died, I got lucky on a piece of land outside of Vegas. Turns out real estate development is a lot about luck."

"Our family never had much."

"Things change. I like to think it was the old man looking out for me from the great beyond." He tapped a finger on his chin. "Do you think he's upstairs or down below given the rat he turned out to be?"

"Shut up, Shep."

"Down below. That's what I think, too. But he's still taking care of me." He shrugged. "I only had to make half a deal with the devil in the process."

"What have you gotten yourself mixed up in now?"

"Success," Shep said, pointing a finger at Cole. "You're not the only one in this family who has something to offer."

"You know better than anyone that I'm no competition in the success game." Cole blew out a breath, rubbed a hand over his jaw. "I'm sheriff in a small town in the middle of the Rocky Mountains. I walked away from a career in the army because I didn't want to deal with Dad's legacy haunting me every step of the way. It works for me, but there's nothing about my life you need to envy."

"I don't envy you," Shep said tightly. "But those stupid two minutes you had on me at birth meant I had to spend my whole childhood in your shadow."

"Not tru—"

"I'm here, Cole. I'm not leaving."

The ridiculous old Western movie phrase "this town ain't big enough for the two of us" leaped into Cole's mind. He felt like he was six years old again, arguing over who got first dibs with their favorite Lego set. But this was his brother. Cole had learned as a kid that all he had to do was wait and Shep would get bored and move on to the next shiny toy.

Somehow Shep had gotten a burr up his backside to mess with Cole again, just when things were starting to feel like a decent fit. Cole wondered if it was that twin spidey sense at work. Shep had somehow recognized Cole's contentment and decided it was high time to crash it.

"Welcome to Crimson," Cole said, making his tone casual. "Folks around here are thrilled the resort's going to open again. It'll mean more jobs for locals and an influx of tourist dollars that the town can always use. A lot of people will be counting on you."

Shep blanched but didn't respond. He'd never been one for responsibility, and Cole knew it.

"You still have my cell number?"

"Yeah, I've got it."

"Give me a call later." Cole flashed a quick smile. "I'll introduce you to Jase Crenshaw, Crimson's mayor. I'm sure he'll want you involved in the local business owners' association right away."

"Sure," Shep agreed, but his voice wavered the tiniest bit.

"Do you have a general contractor lined up?"

Shep stared at him for a long moment, as if he couldn't quite figure out why Cole had changed tactics. Finally he said, "We have plans. Big ones."

"I bet."

"It's not a joke."

"I'm not laughing." Cole gestured to the darkened lodge. "I gather you're not staying here."

"Not yet," Shep admitted. "There's some work to do before the place is habitable again. And I have other... commitments right now."

"What's your time frame?"

"Six months."

"Are you joking? You'll never get things going again in that amount of time."

Shep bristled, as if Cole doubting him was a physical blow. "We're farther along than you think."

Cole ran a hand through his hair. "Why didn't you contact me earlier?"

"I like surprises," Shep said, his smirk firmly back in place.

"Don't cause trouble. This town means something to me, and I won't have you stirring things up around here."

"You sure do know how to make a man feel welcome. It warms my heart. Really."

Cole shook his head, both unable and unwilling to bridge the distance between him and his brother. "I'll see you later, Shep," he said and walked away.

Sienna heard a crash, then another, coming from the kitchen as she walked down the inn's staircase the next morning.

It was too early for construction workers, so she hurried toward the sound, calling out to Paige as she did.

She found the innkeeper grabbing pans and metal bowls from the pantry and slamming them onto the counter.

"Everything okay?"

"Coffee in the pot and French toast casserole on the stove," Paige said, her frenetic movements not stopping. "Do you want fresh squeezed orange juice to go with it?"

"Paige." Sienna put a hand on her friend's arm. "What are you doing?"

"Taking care of the only guest this place might ever see." Paige shook her head and pressed the back of her hand to her mouth when a small sob escaped.

"What are you talking about?"

"I called my mom this morning." Her voice was miserable. "I told you the house is in her name, and I've been trying to save money to buy it from her. I've also been paying the mortgage, and maybe I missed a couple of months because of other expenses I've had to shell out to maintain this place. Maybe I told her I'd miss this month, as well."

"Okay."

"Not okay," Paige countered. "At least that's what I realized. My mom is under contract to sell The Bumblebee."

"She can't do that," Sienna said immediately. "You've put so much time and effort into it. You're almost ready to open."

Paige gave a strained laugh and gestured to the mess of the living room floor. "Not quite almost, but I was getting there. I called to give her an update and talk about the construction expenses. She told me she was approached last week by a buyer out of California who wanted this property."

"Why The Bumblebee?"

"It's not just the house. The land borders the old ski resort. Apparently whoever bought the resort wants to make the inn part of that property. Grammy was always at odds with the former owner of the ski mountain, but I never thought it would be an issue for me."

"Your mom didn't bother to mention this to you?"

Paige sniffed and shook her head. "I made the mistake of calling her in a moment of weakness—when I was feeling overwhelmed. I might have cried and told her I wasn't sure I could handle the inn."

"Crying is okay and doubts are normal. It doesn't mean—"

"I was sick as a kid," Paige blurted. "Really sick."

Sienna felt her mouth drop open. "Are you sick now?"

Paige shook her head. "I had leukemia. I was in and out of the hospital my last two years of high school doing chemo and radiation. I've been fine for almost ten years, but after that phone call, my mom decided that the stress of opening and running an inn would be too much for me." She threw up her hands. "According to her, she's doing me a favor."

"We need to convince her to cancel the sale. When is the closing scheduled?"

"You have no idea what my mom is like when she sets her mind to something."

"Maybe not," Sienna agreed. "However, I'm familiar with overbearing mothers."

Paige gave a soft laugh. "I suppose you are. But you've made a success of yourself in your own right. You have that important job—"

"Which I don't miss."

"You lived with your boyfriend—"

"Who cheated on me," Sienna pointed out with a wince.

"There were some setbacks," Paige admitted. "But you've proven you can be an adult. Before I came to Crimson, I still lived with my mom. She said the house was too big for her to be there alone after my dad died, and she wasn't ready to sell it. The truth was she didn't trust me on my own. Do you have any idea what it's like when no one believes you can handle your own life? It's embarrassing, and now this happens."

Sienna could relate to Paige's dilemma. Maybe her life wasn't as sheltered, but she'd followed wherever her mom and stepdad had led her. Yes, she had a great job, but she'd gotten hired with the ad agency because her step-dad had been fraternity brothers with one of the senior partners. Her mom had basically set up her first date with Kevin through someone she'd met at a charity dinner.

Everything in Sienna's life had been arranged to follow the path that Dana deemed appropriate. As if Sienna couldn't be trusted to make her own decisions.

It wasn't until she'd arrived in Crimson that she'd tasted real freedom. Cole had been the first person to act like he believed she was strong enough to handle whatever life threw at her. No wonder she'd fallen for him so fast and hard. Butterflies flitted around her insides at the thought of him, but right now she needed to focus on seeing her friend through this mini meltdown.

"Your mom lives in Denver, right?" she asked.

"On the south end of town."

"Has she been up here to see what you've done with the place?"

"No. She hasn't been here since my grandma's funeral and the house was a mess at that point. When Grammy died, Mom wanted to sell the inn right away. I convinced her to let me try to make something of it."

"You have," Sienna said immediately, her heart aching to see the other woman so sad. In the past couple of weeks, Paige had become a true friend. They'd spent hours sitting on the front porch at night, and Paige had been infinitely patient listening to all of Sienna's worries. Paige had seemed so settled and sure, and it was a shock to hear about her illness and the uncertainty surrounding her mother and the inn.

"Not quite. I should have known better than to share my problems with her. She's always treated me like the sick girl I used to be, even after I wasn't sick anymore. It's part of the reason I wanted to open the inn. I wanted to prove to her and to myself that I could succeed in something big. I can work hard and it won't hurt me."

"You're doing great," Sienna insisted. "Invite your mom up, and we'll make sure she changes her mind."

"Maybe I can introduce her to your mother," Paige said with a slight smile. "They can compare notes on their wayward daughters."

Sienna grabbed a coffee mug from the counter. "My mom won't be here long enough for that."

"Are you going back to Chicago with her?"

"She definitely thinks so. I managed to convince her I couldn't leave until tomorrow at the earliest. But we both know I can't ignore my life forever."

"But this is your life, too." Paige handed her a carton of creamer as she poured coffee into the mug. "Maybe it's time to think of making some permanent changes. You have to claim the life you want to live."

Sienna lifted a brow. "Like you're going to claim the inn?"

Paige drew in a tremulous breath, like the question had knocked the wind out of her. Then she pulled two plates from a cabinet, porcelain clattering as she placed them on the counter with unsteady hands.

"French toast first," she said with a too-bright smile. "No one should take back her life on an empty stomach."

Sienna nodded. "I'll get the syrup."

Chapter Seventeen

Sienna flipped the button on her phone to vibrate and shoved the device into her purse as she walked through the hospital doors later that morning.

Her mother had called earlier, but Sienna wanted to speak to her dad before facing Dana and her expectations that Sienna would be leaving Crimson.

She wasn't finished in this sweet little town. Despite her mixed emotions, Colorado was quickly beginning to feel like home. She wouldn't give that up without a fight.

She waved to Dixie at the receptionist's desk and headed for the elevators.

"Your mother hasn't aged a day since she left here," the older woman called. "I recognized her the minute she walked in."

Sienna spun on her heel. "In where?"

Dixie chuckled. "The hospital, of course. She got here about twenty minutes ago."

"Is Jase with her?" Sienna asked, already backing away.

"Haven't seen him."

Dana was alone with Declan. The implications screamed through Sienna's brain, as if she was standing too close to the tracks when a powerful freight train came speeding by. She bypassed the elevator and pushed open the stairwell door, taking the steps two at a time to the third floor.

It was difficult to tell whether her gasping breath was a result of racing up two sets of stairs at altitude or the overwhelming panic at the thought of her parents together.

The door to her father's room was open halfway, and she paused outside to catch her breath, gather her thoughts and try to discern whether any blood had been shed yet.

"We had an agreement, Dec. Nothing has changed."

The sharp edge in her mother's tone wasn't a surprise, but her words certainly were.

"She showed up here. That changed everything." Declan coughed, painful and raspy in a way that couldn't be good for his continued recovery. He sounded out of breath and agitated. Sienna started to interrupt the conversation but stopped as her father spoke again. "What was I supposed to do? Send her away? Reject her to her face?"

"Yes," her mother said, exasperation clear in her tone. "If you want to keep receiving the monthly check, then yes."

Sienna felt like she'd taken a punch to the gut. She reached out and put a hand on the wall to steady herself.

"Let him explain," a quiet voice behind her said.

She turned to find Jase standing a few feet behind her, Emily at his side. Her sister-in-law's gaze was gentle, and Sienna understood she'd been duped by everyone. As far as she'd seen, Emily wasn't one for sympathy...ever.

"I've got to get out of here," she muttered, but her legs were rooted to the polished linoleum floor.

"Sienna?" The door to the room opened to reveal her mother standing stiff as a statue, her mouth pressed into a tight line even as her gaze tracked wildly from Sienna to Jase.

"Baby girl, come in here," Declan called from over Dana's shoulder. "We need to talk."

"Did you pay him to stay away from me?" Sienna didn't move, ignoring her dad's request.

"I helped out with living expenses." Dana glanced at Jase again. "For your brother."

"Sienna!" Declan shouted. "Get her in here."

Dana gave a small nod. "We can discuss the details behind closed doors. No need for the entire hospital to overhear you."

But Sienna was beyond caring who knew this latest detail in their sordid family history. "Did your *help* include an agreement that he wouldn't try to contact me?"

Her mother tipped up her chin and gave Sienna the patented mom stare that used to shut her down when she asked questions about her dad and brother.

Sienna pressed her palm flat against the wall and stared back.

"Your father and I had an understanding. I never forbade him from contacting you."

"The hell you didn't, woman," Declan called from inside the room. "Now someone get me out of this dang bed."

"You had no right," Sienna whispered to her mother.

Dana's eyes narrowed. "He cashed the checks every month."

"Dad had some rough times," Jase explained, stepping forward. "He needed—"

"Did you know about this the whole time?" Sienna

demanded, pulling her hand away from the wall and fisting it at her side.

"Not at first," Jase said after a moment. "But eventually I started managing the bank account."

"Inappropriate to put a child in that situation," Dana muttered.

Sienna felt like she was at the center of a tornado, all the parts of her life spinning around her in a whirlwind.

"Do you want to get a cup of coffee?" Emily asked. "A few minutes away might help you collect your thoughts."

"I don't need time." Sienna looked between the three people facing her. "My thoughts are clear. You've all lied to me. I want nothing to do with any of you."

Sienna paced back and forth in the corner office of the sheriff's department, anger and humiliation buzzing through her like a swarm of insects.

The friendly woman at the front desk had offered her a cup of coffee, then led her to Cole's office. He was on his way back to the station, she'd explained, and Sienna was welcome to wait.

The door burst open a few seconds later, and Cole appeared, his gaze frantic. "Marlene called me," he said, moving toward Sienna. "She said my girlfriend was in the office crying and that I'd better get my butt back here stat."

Sienna's cheeks grew warm as a thrill coursed through her at his casual use of the word *girlfriend*. Did that make her optimistic or pathetic? Probably a bit of both. "I hope she didn't actually use the word *stat*."

"She did," he confirmed. "Marlene's a big fan of medical shows. She's also happy to give an armchair diagnosis of any physical ailments you might have."

"I'll remember that." Sienna smoothed her fingers

across her cheeks. "For the record, I wasn't crying when I got here. I was totally composed when I walked into the station."

"But you'd been crying?" He didn't wait for an answer, only reached for her. His strong arms wound around her back as he pulled her against his chest.

She sucked in a shaky breath and let herself sag against him. They stood together for several minutes, Cole gently tracing circles on her back with his palm. She splayed her fingers across his shirtfront, feeling the steady beat of his heart. The sorrow that had tightened around her chest, ensnaring her heart like a vine, slowly subsided.

It was this moment more than any other that made her certain of her love for him. He felt like home, and she'd been yearning for a place to belong for as long as she could remember. She drew in her first normal breath since leaving the hospital, realizing she could handle anything with this man at her side.

"My mother went to visit my dad in the hospital this morning," she said, pulling away.

As reluctant as she was to leave Cole's embrace, she had to have a little distance to get the words out. She walked to the edge of the desk, ran her fingers along a deep scratch in the oak top.

"I take it things didn't go well."

"Not exactly. They argued over the money she'd been giving him all this time."

Cole's thick brows furrowed, but otherwise he didn't respond. She'd expected him to be as shocked as she was by the revelation so she didn't quite understand his calm reaction to the news.

Maybe he didn't understand the implication of what she was telling him. "Mom has been sending a monthly check to Declan for the past twenty years," she explained. "She tried to tell me it was for Jase, but obviously my brother is a grown man now and even when he was a kid…" She shook her head, confused that Cole still looked unsurprised. "They had an unspoken agreement that Declan wouldn't contact me. Jase knew about it. He'd started depositing the checks when Declan was having issues."

"That's a lot of pressure for a kid," Cole said quietly. "Your parents never should have made that arrangement."

"Yes," she agreed slowly, an uncomfortable feeling—an itch she couldn't quite reach—skittered along the back of her neck. "That's not the point. Jase knew and never mentioned it. My mom made me believe my dad wanted nothing to do with me. Declan took the money and was willing to stay out of my life to ensure it didn't stop. It's untenable that they'd all have kept this from me, even once I arrived in Crimson."

"I'm sorry, Sienna." He crossed his arms over his chest. "It was a bad situation all around. But you have to understand—"

"You knew." She lifted her arm, pointing a finger at him. It felt as though her hand wasn't connected to her body. She saw everything through the haze of heartache crashing over her once again. Only this time it was a pain she doubted she'd ever recover from. "You knew about the checks."

"Jase didn't like keeping it from you." Cole took a step forward but she stretched out her hand, palm out, to keep him from moving closer to her. "He was trying to figure out a way to tell you. He mentioned that Declan hadn't cashed the checks for a while, if that helps."

She felt her eyes widen. "You've discussed this with Jase."

"He needed to confide in someone," Cole said by way of explanation. "It was long before you and I were together."

"We're *not* together," she whispered, the words little pokes of a dagger. Her insides were raw at this point, battered and bloody, and yet the hits just kept on coming.

"Don't say that." He closed his hand around hers but she wrenched away, trying to gather herself. Trying to make sense of any of this. She felt the heat of his body behind her, although he didn't try to touch her again. "This can't come between us. Not now."

"I trusted you, Cole. I love you."

As soon as she said the words, she knew they were a mistake. His features went blank, as if he were suddenly made of stone.

"You must have heard I was a bad bet," he said with no inflection. "You should have listened."

She drew in a breath, squared her shoulders and met his dark gaze. "That's an excuse to keep yourself from being hurt, and we both know it."

"I care about you, Sienna." He shrugged, ran a hand through his hair. "That's all I have to give you."

Care. What an inconsequential word compared to the all-encompassing love she felt for him. Care was a nibble on a corner of stale bread and she was ready to offer the entire buffet—her heart and soul spread out before Cole. She'd wanted to give him everything.

"It isn't enough, and I don't believe it anyway. Not after everything—"

"Jase would have told you about the checks," he interrupted, a clumsy change of subject that made Sienna want to scream in frustration. "Eventually. Or made Declan do it. You shouldn't have found out the way you did."

"Thanks, Sheriff Obvious." Her anger was the rising

tide at the beach on a hot summer day. She let it wash over her, obliterating her heartache—at least for the moment.

It was hard to see Cole as anything but the man she loved, so Sienna let anger surge through her heart. The less she allowed herself to feel right now, the more she could handle without a total breakdown.

"I'm sorry," he said, lifting a hand as if to reach for her again, then dropping it when she took another step away.

"Me, too," she whispered, her hand on the door to his office. "You'll never know how much."

"Make it right, Jase."

Cole didn't need to turn around on the barstool where he'd been planted for the past two hours to know his friend had arrived at Elevation Brewery, the most popular bar in Crimson. Guilt radiated from Jase, hot and sticky, scorching everything in its path.

"Tell me how." Jase took a seat next to him and inclined his head to the man behind the bar. "Hey, David. Gimme whatever the sheriff's drinking."

"Too much whiskey," David McCay, the bar's owner, said quietly.

Out of the corner of his eye, Cole saw Jase nod. "Sounds good to me."

David frowned but pulled a bottle of Jack Daniels from the shelf behind the bar. "Is there some high altitude apocalypse on the horizon?" he asked as he poured two fingers into a highball glass and set it in front of Jase. "Because it concerns me to see two of our top town leaders bellied up to my bar looking like they just got kicked in the family jewels."

"His fault." Cole hitched a thumb toward Jase. "He's a damn liar."

Jase grimaced. "Mind dialing down the volume? That's the last thing I need broadcast out to the town."

"A coward, too," Cole added, ratcheting up his voice another notch. "I'm only telling the truth here. You should try it sometime, Mr. Mayor."

"How much has he had?" Jase asked David.

"Enough that I'm cutting him off after that one."

Jase leaned toward Cole. "Ida Wasinski is devouring a plate of wings at the table to your left. She's the biggest gossip in Crimson, and she's watching you like you're covered in buffalo sauce."

"You can't cut me off." The burn of the alcohol was the only thing that could ease the stabbing pain in his heart. Cole drained his glass, then pushed it toward David. "You think I'm going to be arrested if I have another drink?"

David shook his head. "I think you're going to keep running your mouth, which might be worse."

"Bring the lawman a drink, barkeep."

Cole groaned as Shep slapped him on the shoulder.

David's eyes widened and he swore under his breath. Jase swiveled his seat so he was facing the two Bennett brothers.

"That must have been one hell of a pour," he said, glancing toward his empty glass. "Because I'm seeing double."

"Not for long," Cole muttered. "Get out of here, Shep."

"In your dreams." Shep settled on the barstool next to Cole. "I take it my brother the sheriff didn't spend his off-duty hours regaling you with clever anecdotes from our twinsie childhood."

"They know about you."

"Hypothetical knowing and real-life seeing are different things," Jase said, rubbing a hand over his eyes.

"Put your faces next to each other's so I can compare your features."

Cole rolled his eyes. "Kiss my—"

"Another round for everyone," David said quickly. He poured liquor into three glasses, then got called to the other end of the bar.

"My brother," Shep said, leaning back to speak directly to Jase, "never loses control."

Jase held up his glass as if he was toasting Cole's self-control. "He's a steady force in this community. A real prize."

"A prize," Cole muttered with a sharp laugh. "Gee, thanks."

"Which makes whatever's going on tonight all the more intriguing." Shep tapped a finger on his chin as if he was pondering the future of the world. Cole wanted to punch him.

"What brings you to Crimson, Shep?" Jase asked.

Cole might be damn angry with his best friend, but he could still appreciate that Jase was trying to distract Shep. Cole sure as hell didn't want to share anything about his feelings for Sienna with his twin. Even without details and not factoring alcohol into the equation, Shep had to be able to sense how upset Cole was and that meant giving his brother too much power.

"I bought some property here."

"A summer home?"

"Not exactly."

"The ski resort," Cole blurted, sick of Shep's weird little head games.

"Thanks, bro," Shep whispered.

"It's not like it's a secret."

Jase's mouth dropped open but he quickly closed it. "You're with the Trinity Development Company?"

"I'm the president."

"Well then, welcome to Crimson."

"You're the mayor, right?"

"I am."

"And friends with my brother."

"Yes," Jase said at the same time Cole mumbled, "We'll see."

"Trouble in paradise?" One side of Shep's mouth curved. "Did one of you lads break the bro code? Skim a little from the other's milk?"

"Shut up, Shep."

"Nothing like that," Jase clarified. "It's my sister."

"You dishonored a friend's sister?" Shep nudged Cole's shoulder. "I didn't think you had it in you, buddy."

"Do you ever get sick of being a jerk?" Cole asked his brother.

"Nope," Shep said with a laugh. "It's my superpower."

"A jerk is handling the reopening of the ski mountain?" Jase downed the remainder of his drink. "Perfect."

"Sienna is the only thing I care about right now." Cole leaned his elbows on the bar and bent his head forward. "You should have seen how she looked at me."

Jase sighed. "I know exactly how she looked at you because it was the same way with me."

"Not the same," Cole muttered. "You're not in love with her."

Shep whistled low under his breath.

"Hell, no, I'm not *in* love with her. She's my sis—" Jase stopped, sucked a breath. "Did you say you're in love with her? With my sister?"

"That explains everything," Shep said. He took another sip of whiskey. "If you love this chick, then of course you messed it up."

"She's not a chick," Cole snapped, then turned to his brother. "Don't call her that."

"Yeah," Jase agreed. "Show some respect."

Shep held up his hands. "Got it."

"What do you mean, of course I messed it up?"

"Tell me what happened."

Cole pressed his lips together. "There was something she didn't know that I knew and when she realized I knew before she knew—"

"He lied to her." Jase rose from his stool.

"I didn't lie," Cole countered. "I just didn't tell her that you'd lied."

"It was for her own good," Jase said, shaking his head.

"I thought so, too," Cole said.

"Like all of Dad's lies were for Mom's own good?" Shep asked.

Cole shook his head. "Don't go there."

"Isn't that what he told her?" Shep took another long drink. "That's what he told all of us." His tone was disgusted. "He ruined her." He tipped his glass toward Cole. "And this ch...woman probably got off easy. How long were you together anyway?"

"It doesn't matter," Cole said. "What matters is that I should have told her from the start."

"What was the big lie anyway?" Shep asked.

Cole glanced toward Jase, who shrugged.

"There was something she didn't know about the agreement her parents had for child support after they got divorced," Cole said.

Jase laughed softly. "You should be the politician. That was the biggest spin I've ever heard." He took a step toward Shep. "My mother moved away from Crimson with Sienna when we were kids. My dad was a mess. Mom sent him money, and it was understood that he wouldn't contact her or see my sister."

"Like a payoff?" Shep asked.

"Such an ugly word," Jase muttered.

"Exactly like a payoff," Cole admitted, even though he'd tried to convince himself it was something different when Jase had first told him about the arrangement.

"That's bad." Shep leaned forward over the bar. "Bartender," he shouted. "Another round for these two idiots and one for me, as well."

Cole looked to David and shook his head slightly. "No more for me." He glanced at his brother. "It's bad."

"Why didn't you tell her?"

"I'm an idiot," Cole muttered. "Just like you said."

"It's my fault." Jase shook his head. "I asked you not to say anything."

Shep gave a small laugh. "Bros before—"

"Sometimes I wish we were twelve again," Cole interrupted, "so I could tackle you to the ground. It's better this way. She got out early before I could hurt her even worse than I have. I'm my father's son after all."

"You don't actually believe that."

Cole glanced at his brother. "What are you talking about? We look just like him."

"I'm not debating paternity." Shep ran a hand through his hair. "But you aren't like him." He leaned in closer. "You are *not* our father."

"I lied to her," Cole whispered.

"Yes, and you'll have to fix the mess you're in. I recommend flowers and jewelry and a load of sappy, humiliating groveling. You can make this better. Hell, Cole, Dad could have made it better if he hadn't been such a coward."

"He was going to jail."

"Which didn't stop Mom from loving him. He gave up on her and on himself. That's the part I couldn't face. That's why I never came back. He was supposed to be the strongest man I knew, and he gave up. Don't be like him. Don't give up."

"I hate to side with your brother," Jase said, "but he's right."

"Hell, yeah, I am." Shep stood from his chair, pulled his wallet from his back pocket and threw a few crisp bills on the bar. "Do you know why?" He held up a hand before Cole could answer. "Because *you* are the strongest man I know. It sounds like this woman loves you, and there is nothing worth fighting for more important than that. Speaking of, I've actually got a lady waiting on me tonight. You two sad saps remind me I'd rather be with her."

"I thought you just got to town," Jase murmured. "You work fast."

Shep flashed a grin. "Something like that."

Cole met his brother's gaze, and it was like looking at a version of his own reflection. "I'm glad you're here," he said quietly, surprised to realize it had been true from the first moment he'd spotted Shep on the ski resort's patio. His brother might infuriate him, but their bond couldn't be broken.

"Besides…" Shep quickly drained the glass of whiskey David had set on the bar in front of him, then took two steps back. "If you don't handle it, I'm going to have to make myself available to help this poor girl get over you."

"Shut up."

"See ya, Cole." Shep turned with a laugh and walked out of the bar.

"Can I fix this?" Cole asked Jase a moment later.

His friend sighed. "I sure as hell hope so."

Chapter Eighteen

Sienna looked up from the suitcase she was packing the next morning, shocked to see her father standing in the doorway of her room in the inn.

"You were discharged?" she asked, pressing a hand to her chest.

Declan shrugged. "AMA."

Sienna felt her mouth drop open. "Against medical advice? Dad, you can't do that. You have to go back. Let me take you back."

He inclined his head toward the window at the front of the house. "I'm paying the cabbie to wait. Johnny and me have been friends forever. He cleaned up his act a few years before me, but he understands what I'm trying to do here."

"Which is?" she asked slowly.

"Make things right," he answered, flashing one of his self-deprecating grins. The years might have been hard on her father but she could see the handsome man he must have been twenty years ago. It was no wonder her mother had found him irresistible. "Can I come in?"

"You need to be in the hospital."

"They were going to release me eventually." He lifted a brow. "This won't take long, baby girl, but you have every right to send me away if that's what you need to do. Lord knows I deserve it."

Sienna closed her eyes for a moment. A part of her wanted to refuse to hear him out. She had a flight booked to Chicago that afternoon, even though she didn't recognize the life she was returning to. Her mother had left Crimson last night. She'd tried to convince Sienna she'd sent the monthly checks for Jase's benefit and not to bribe Declan to stay out of Sienna's life. Sienna didn't believe it, but where else did she have to go at this point?

At least she had a history in Chicago. A job and friends…although the connections she'd made during her short time in Crimson felt just as strong as the relationships she'd had for years.

"I've got five minutes," she said, meeting her father's slate blue gaze.

"I only need four," he promised and stepped into the room.

He took a thick envelope from his back pocket and shoved it toward her. "Johnny ran me by the house before we came here," he explained. "This is for you."

She shook her head. "I don't want your money."

"Darlin', I don't have any money," he said, then laughed. "Just open the envelope. Please."

She took it, and they both ignored her trembling fingers.

"Why?" she whispered, glancing between her father and the thick stack of checks in the envelope. They were made out to Declan, written in her mother's precise script. Each one was dated for the first of the month, and they went back over ten years.

"Your mother sent them even after Jase graduated high school." He lifted one shoulder, let it drop like the weight on it was too much to sustain. "I was in pretty bad shape at that point, and she knew it. She sent a note—it was the first communication other than the checks I'd had with her since she left with you."

Despite Sienna's anger, the pain in her dad's voice tore at her heart. Was it any wonder she was so messed up in her own life when she had the parents she did? Declan and Dana made dysfunction anything but fun. "You don't have to share this with me." She didn't want to hear it. She didn't want to feel anything for this man.

"She told me to use the money to get my act together," he continued as if she hadn't spoken. Sienna got the impression he was saying the words as much for his own benefit as hers. "Because if you ever came looking for me, she wanted me to be around to deserve a second chance with you."

Sienna shook her head slowly. "I don't believe it." The checks felt like a flame in her hand. It burned through her skin, but she kept her fingers tight on the edge of the stack. She couldn't let go just yet. "She didn't want me to see you. She hated when I came here."

"Can you blame her?" he asked. "I don't. Of course your mom didn't want you anywhere near me, but she still wanted what was best for you."

"So why didn't you cash the checks?" She held up the envelope. "What's the point of saving them?"

"That note was a wake-up call." He scratched at the stubble that covered his jaw and smiled again. "Not that I was ready to wake up just then, but it resonated with me. I didn't want to owe getting clean to your mom. I wanted to earn my way back into your life on my own."

"But you never contacted me," she countered. "Even after you got sober."

"Letting you go was my greatest regret," he said quietly. "Don't think I didn't realize what kind of a father it made me, even if I could rationalize it at the time. I still don't deserve to be a part of your life, Sienna."

"Why did you let Jase stay?" It was the question that still plagued her. Why was her brother important enough to keep when she could be so easily discarded?

"He was different." Declan shrugged. "It's not logical, but the Crenshaws had been a family of boys for generations. Bad boys that turned into lousy men. I figured Jase could handle anything that came down the pike because it was in his blood. But you…" He sighed, his eyes drifting closed. "You were different. You were this bright, shiny thing in the cesspool of my life. A girl. The first one with the name Crenshaw in three generations. The thought of what could happen to you in this town…" He threw up his hands. "Your mom was right to take you away."

"I still don't believe that. Not the way she did it— letting me think you didn't want me." She took a breath, then added, "That you didn't love me."

"I always loved you," he said, moving forward. "I always will, baby girl. Whether you're in Crimson or Chicago or halfway around the world."

She bit down on the inside of her cheek to keep from crying. She *would not* cry.

"Do what you want with those checks," he said, covering her hand with his. "I never understood why I was saving them, but now I know it was to give them to you. You can hate me and refuse to speak to me but don't ever doubt that I love you." The corner of his mouth lifted. "In my own messed-up way."

She choked back a sob. "Is there any other way to love someone?"

He pulled her in for a tight hug. "Not in this family," he said.

After a moment, Sienna relaxed into him, and it felt like coming home.

Sienna watched the black Porsche tear into the ski resort's empty parking lot. Dust flew up around the SUV as it came to a quick stop in front of where she sat on the gravel.

She sucked in a breath as a man rushed from the vehicle, slamming shut the driver's side door and stalking toward her. Shep Bennett was indeed identical in looks to Cole, although Sienna would never confuse one brother for the other. She'd been shocked when Paige had told her Shep's company had bought the ski resort and that he was personally under contract to purchase The Bumblebee.

Of course, she couldn't call Cole to ask him about it because she wasn't speaking to Cole—wasn't sure if she'd ever speak to him again. She knew it didn't make sense, but the fact that he hadn't told her what he knew about her parents' arrangement felt like a bigger betrayal than her family lying to her all those years. Although she knew in her heart—her broken heart—the lie was just an excuse.

"You're trespassing, Sienna." He pointed a finger at her. "Not to mention making me think my resort was on fire and scaring the hell out of me."

Sienna looked up at the plume of smoke wafting into the air, then poked a stick at the smoldering logs in the metal fire pit she'd dragged from around the back of the lodge.

"You know who I am," she said quietly.

Shep nodded. "My brother is pretty much tied in knots over you. I'll admit I was curious, although he forgot to mention your pyromaniac tendencies. You know there's a fire ban around here?"

"That's why I'm in the parking lot, where there are no trees. It seemed safe." She glanced at Shep and raised a brow. "Are you going to call the cops?"

Shep blew out a breath. "Sadly, you don't look like a handcuffs type of girl."

"You have no idea what kind of woman I am."

"The kind my brother fell in love with, which says something about you."

"That I was crazy," Sienna muttered, "to get involved with him."

"Well, yes," Shep agreed, rubbing a hand over his jaw in a gesture so similar to Cole's that it made her heart ache. He glanced back at the SUV, then crouched down next to her. "What's with the fire?"

"Maybe I wanted to make s'mores."

"Or burn down the forest." He grabbed the stick from her hand. "Enough poking at it. You got your point across."

"Back off, Smokey Bear," she said under her breath.

Shep laughed. "I can see why Cole is so damn in love with you."

She leveled a glare at him. "Your brother said he *cares* about me, which is not the same thing as love."

"Not always silky smooth, that guy. I also heard he lied to you, although he wasn't forthcoming with much in the way of details."

"I've got the details right here." Sienna plucked another check out of the envelope she held between her knees, wadded it into a ball, then tossed it into the fire. The edges caught first, burning bright orange, then turning to black as the paper disintegrated in the heat of the fire.

She'd come out to the ski resort because she wanted to be alone but didn't trust her rental car on the dirt roads that led into Forest Service land. The mountains were so close here it felt like they were embracing the valley, and it surprised her that no one had bought the property sooner.

Shep straightened when a noise came from the SUV. He jogged around the driver's side and Sienna heard a small cry, then the soft rumble of Shep making soothing sounds.

"Tell me you don't have a baby in that Porsche," she called as she stood.

"Rosie will actually be eighteen months next week," Shep said as he reappeared, a child snuggled to his chest. "She's officially a toddler."

Sienna felt her mouth drop open. "Where did you get her?"

"Aisle seven of the local grocery," Shep answered with a wink. "Near the canned peas."

"Shep."

He moved forward, smoothing fine, dark hair away from Rosie's face. "Rosie is my daughter."

"Does Cole know?"

Shep shook his head, his full lips thinning. "Not yet. Hell, I didn't even know about her until recently."

"You shouldn't curse in front of a child," Sienna said automatically.

"Thanks for the tip," Shep said tightly. "I'll add it to the list of things I need to learn about being a dad." He cupped a hand on the back of Rosie's head. "It's a long damn list."

"Shep."

He groaned. "No cursing. Right."

"Dada," Rosie said in a tiny voice. She tipped up her face to look at Shep. "Damn, Dada."

"I'm a bad daddy." Shep dropped a kiss on the tip of the young girl's nose. "I'll do better next time."

"That's why no cursing," Sienna told him, unable to hide her smile. "Hi, Rosie."

Rosie shifted in her father's arms, looked at Sienna, then buried her face in Shep's shirtfront.

"She's kind of shy," Shep offered. "Plus she fell asleep in the car, and it takes her a while to wake up from a nap. Takes after her daddy in that respect. This is Sienna," he explained to his daughter. "She's a friend of your uncle Cole's. I told you about him, remember? He looks like Daddy, only not as handsome."

After a moment, Rosie turned to look at Sienna again, her gaze wary. The girl was adorable, with big brown eyes and dark hair that curled above her ears. She wore a wrinkled pink dress and polka-dot socks on her feet.

"Is it just the two of you?" Sienna asked.

"I brought a nanny with us from California, but she took off this morning." Shep rolled his eyes. "Saw a bear on her run and freaked out."

"She just left?"

"So fast it would make your head spin."

"Jettie," Rosie said with a sniff.

"Jessie had to go back to Los Angeles," Shep said with a sigh. "Where there are way scarier things on the streets than bears if you ask me."

"You need help."

"No doubt," Shep agreed. "But the first thing I need is for you to completely put out that fire."

"Got it." Sienna picked up the bucket of water she'd

set to one side of the fire pit. "I was prepared. I really wasn't trying to cause trouble." She closed her eyes for a moment as the memory of Cole teasing about her being a troublemaker played through her mind.

Shep eyed the now empty envelope on the ground. "What exactly were you doing? I can't imagine Cole writing love letters for you to burn."

The wood sizzled as she dumped the bucket of water over it, a huge rush of smoke pouring into the air.

Rosie covered her ears and shouted, "'Moke, Daddy."

"It's okay, sweetheart. I've got you." Shep stepped back toward the SUV.

When the smoke cleared, Sienna turned to Cole's brother. "Just getting rid of some old family drama."

"Cole and I have plenty of that ourselves," Shep told her. "Next time, drown your sorrows at a bar like he did. It's a lot safer for all of us."

She picked up the envelope and crumpled it into a ball as Shep opened the door and loaded Rosie into her car seat. "Cole had *sorrows* to drown?"

"Oh, yeah. He was a bad drunk and that *never* happens to my brother. I'm sure whatever he did to mess things up was bad, but I can guarantee he regrets it. I hope you give him another chance." He shut the door and flashed a wide grin. "I have a feeling he'll be a lot easier to deal with if you're a part of his life. I know I would be."

Sienna gave a small wave as Shep climbed in the Porsche and drove away. Her feelings were still jumbled enough that she wasn't sure she wanted another chance with Cole. She could easily forgive him for not telling her about the checks. But she'd told him she loved him and he'd offered her nothing in return.

After spending most of her life wondering if she was

even worthy of love, Sienna had finally realized she deserved so much more than she'd ever believed. And she was no longer willing to settle for someone who'd give her anything less.

Chapter Nineteen

"Isn't there some kind of limit on how many turns a person can take with this thing?" Cole climbed back onto the dunk tank platform at the Crimson Fourth of July Festival the following weekend, pushed sopping wet hair away from his face.

"It's for charity, boss," Marlene called from the ticket table she was manning next to the booth. She held up the cash box in his direction. "We're making lots of money for the community center."

"Yeah, Sheriff. Don't be a bad sport."

Cole glared at his brother, who was gleefully handing over another five-dollar bill to Marlene.

"I'm a great sport," Cole argued, gathering the hem of his uniform shirt in his hands to wring out the water. It had been Marlene's idea that he wear the uniform, but he'd refused the sign she'd tried to hand him that read Did I Give You a Ticket? No sense in giving the festival-goers too much motivation.

He glanced up at the clear sky, grateful for another bluebird day in Colorado. At least he had the sunshine to warm him between dunks, although thanks to the ice-cold water in the tank, he was still shivering slightly. "But you're taking too much pleasure in soaking me."

"Just loosening up the arm," Shep said with a laugh, shifting his hold on Rosie. "You want to see Daddy dunk Uncle Cole again, sweetheart?"

Rosie clapped her chubby hands. "Dunk, Daddy!"

"Good idea." Cole pointed toward Shep through the bars of the dunk tank. "Why don't we change places?"

"Not a chance. Besides, the good people of Crimson want to see their fine, upstanding sheriff take the plunge, not his newcomer brother." Shep turned to the crowd that had gathered in front of the dunk tank, tossing a ball in the air. "Isn't that right, everyone?"

A round of cheers went up and Cole gave an obligatory smile and wave.

The festival was in full swing. Booths housing carnival games and food trucks lined the perimeter of the field next to the county fairgrounds outside of town. An oversize tent with picnic tables under it and a large stage were situated at one end of the festivities, and a three-piece bluegrass band played to an audience of older folks and families.

But the big draw this afternoon was the dunking booth, especially since Cole had climbed onto the platform thirty minutes ago. He'd replaced Jase, who'd only had a few people interested in dunking him. Cole, on the other hand, was a popular target.

First up had been Emily, then Katie Crawford, then Declan. Cole was pretty sure Sienna's father would have rather aimed the ball directly at Cole's head, but the old man managed to send him into the tank of freezing water on the first throw. Impressive for a man still recovering from a stint in the hospital.

Cole hadn't complained or tried to defend himself against Sienna's little posse of protectors. He wanted to fix the mess he'd made.

He'd even paid a visit to Declan's house after he'd learned Sienna had moved in to help take care of her father. Declan had seemed to take great pleasure in slamming the door shut in Cole's face. Cole hadn't slept in a week, had no appetite and could barely focus on work as his thoughts were consumed with Sienna and how to win her back. But earning a second chance was difficult when she apparently wanted nothing to do with him.

"I'd like to dunk the newcomer," a voice called out now, and Cole watched the sea of bystanders part to reveal Paige Harper glaring at Shep.

"It's about time," Cole muttered under his breath. "I need a break."

"I've got a baby in my arms," Shep said, glancing over his shoulder at Cole, then back to Paige. "Miss, I'm not sure what I've done to raise your ire, but I can assure you—"

"Save it, buddy." She plucked the ball from Shep's fingers. "Cute kid, by the way."

Cole couldn't help but smile at the shocked look on Shep's face as Paige leaned in to tickle Rosie's dimpled chin. The little girl, who was the shyest child Cole had ever encountered, giggled and reached for Paige.

"Stay with your daddy," Paige said, smoothing a hand across Rosie's soft hair. "I have business with your uncle Cole, too."

Rosie flashed a toothy grin, then shoved her fist into her mouth.

Cole had never seen his brother at a loss for words,

but Shep stared at Paige like she was standing there juggling in nothing but her birthday suit.

Paige stepped forward, eyeing the ball in her hand. "How much for a guaranteed dunk?" she asked Marlene.

"That's not part of the deal," Cole shouted. "She has to hit the target."

"I'll hit it all right," Paige shouted back. "But I'll wish it were your face."

Shep let out a low moan. "A toddler whisperer with a temper? I think I've died and gone to heaven."

"I tried calling her but she won't answer," Cole said to Paige, leaning forward as if that would prevent the rest of the town from hearing his words. He'd made a habit of keeping his private life just that, but somehow everyone in Crimson seemed to know that things had gone south between Sienna and him. Hard to believe, when it had been only a few weeks since he'd stopped her on the road from Aspen, but that's how small towns worked. Nothing was private in Crimson. Not for long anyway.

"Ten dollars," Marlene told Paige, who quickly pulled a few bills from her purse.

"Done," she said, slapping them on the table, then stalking toward Cole. "You should try harder."

"Tell me how."

She gave a small shake of her head, curls bouncing. "You don't deserve to know. I told you she needed someone in her corner."

"I know you did." Cole swiped a hand across his eyes, sweat beginning to bead along his forehead despite the cool breeze whirling across the fairgrounds. "I should have been that person."

"But you weren't." Paige yelled the words despite the fact that she was standing right next to the dunk tank.

"You broke her heart. You hurt her. Do you know that she almost—?"

"Paige."

The tiny woman clasped a hand over her mouth and turned as Sienna walked out of the crowd.

"Almost what?" Cole asked, leaning forward. He sucked in a breath as Sienna moved toward the dunk tank. She wore a red floral shirt with lace detailing around the neckline and slim denim jeans that molded over her curves in a way that made his mouth go dry. Her long hair was down, casually curling over her shoulders. She looked so beautiful, happy and at peace in a way he hadn't seen before.

Then she met his gaze and the pain in her eyes was like a gunshot to his heart because he knew he'd put it there.

"You don't have to do this," she said, her gaze gentling as she looped an arm around Paige's shoulder. "As much as I appreciate it—"

"I have pent-up aggression," Paige muttered, darting a glare toward Shep. "And I can't take it out on the brother holding the kid. Cole's an easier target."

"Literally," Cole said, then shrugged when both women turned to him. "I'm stuck in this cage and half the town has some sort of bizarre need to defend your honor."

"I'm heading to the beer tent," Paige said, giving Sienna a quick hug. "Meet me there."

Sienna nodded, then tipped up her chin as she focused on Cole once again. "I can take care of myself."

"I know you can," he whispered, loving how color flooded her cheeks even as she glared at him. Loving everything about her. Offering up a thousand silent prayers that she'd give him another chance—one he wouldn't squander.

"I almost left Crimson," she said, crossing her arms

over her chest. "That's what Paige was about to tell you. As much as I wanted to, I didn't think I could stand to stay and risk running into you and pretend like things were right between us."

"I want us to be right."

She shifted to look back at the crowd of people watching them. His brother. Her brother and Emily. Declan. Marlene. A dozen other people he knew in some capacity. His most colossal mistake on display for everyone to witness, and he still had no idea how to make it better.

He met his brother's dark gaze, watching Shep's eyes widen as he inclined his head toward Sienna like he was trying to tell Cole something. Shep raised a hand and pointed a finger toward his eye then lowered it to his chest and finally leveled it at Cole.

Eye. Heart. You.

I love you.

Cole still hadn't said the words out loud, although he'd replayed them in his head countless times over the past week.

"Sienna."

She swiped a hand across her cheek. "I can't do this now," she said softly and took a step away.

"Wait." He leaned forward so fast he almost slipped off the platform. "Don't go. Please. I need to talk to you. I need to tell you I love you."

A chorus of cheers went up from the people watching, and Sienna froze. Cole waited for what seemed like an eternity until she finally lifted an arm, as if she were holding out her hand to him. Instead she reached forward and casually pressed the dunk tank lever.

Sienna watched Cole drop into the tank with a splash, droplets of frigid water hitting her face and shoulders.

He surfaced a moment later, sputtering and wiping water from his eyes.

"I tell you I love you," he said, coughing violently, "and you dunk me?"

She shook her head and took a step back. "I dunked you for breaking my heart in the first place."

He stilled for a moment, then grabbed onto the bars of the cage and pulled himself forward. "I'm sorry."

"Dunk him again," a man from the crowd shouted.

"Shut up, Shep," Cole shouted back, then unlatched the cage and started out of the tank.

"You have five minutes left on your time, Sheriff," Marlene called.

"I'll donate a hundred dollars to the community center as a forfeit," Cole said, hoisting himself over the metal side. Water sluiced from his body and his sheriff's uniform clung to the hard muscles of his chest and thighs. Sienna had a ridiculous thought of Poseidon emerging from the sea.

Cole was a god in that moment and she was a mere mortal and how could she resist a god? His words had cut through the newly built defenses she'd erected around her heart, and she automatically turned away, afraid of how much she wanted them to be true.

He circled her wrist with his hand. "Please don't go."

His fingers were icy cold, but she could still feel the heat of his body behind her, and she wanted nothing more than to turn and wrap herself around him and never let go.

"I'm staying because this is my home," she said, keeping her gaze straight ahead. "I belong here. I made that decision for me and no one else."

He shifted his grasp on her arm, sliding his fingers across her hand and interlacing them with hers. "You're my home," he said quietly. "I belong anywhere you are,

Sienna. I'm sorry I was too much of an idiot to tell you that when you needed to hear it."

"Me, too," she whispered.

Ignoring the crowd still watching them, he moved in front of her, keeping their hands linked together. "I'm saying it now, sweetheart. I love you with everything I am and if you give me another chance, I'll prove it to you every day for the rest of our lives. I know you don't need me. You're so damn strong, and I can't tell you how happy it makes me that you finally know it."

She drew in a breath. "You helped me understand that," she admitted. "I'm not sure I would have believed it about myself if you hadn't believed it first."

"There was never a doubt in my mind." He stepped closer, crowding her a little. "I know I hurt you, and I probably don't deserve your forgiveness. I'm not the sharpest knife in the drawer, but I can learn. I finally understand that I have to take some risks to get the life I want. A true home and a family—someone who will make my life complete. You, Sienna. I want you and I get that I have to be brave to earn my place at your side."

She laughed as hope filled her, making her feel lighter than she had in years. "You know how to be brave. You're the sheriff."

"Not with my heart," he told her. "Not until you. If you want me to walk away—"

She pressed her fingers to his lips. "Don't you dare."

"I'll never go far," he finished quickly. "There's no place I can imagine being except by your side." He traced his thumb against the inside of her wrist, his touch sending shivers of awareness across her skin.

"I love you, Cole," she whispered, then yelped as he lifted her in his arms and gathered her close. "But you're a soaking wet mess."

"I'm your mess," he said. "Forever if you'll have me." He pressed his mouth to hers, the kiss at once tender and possessive. She was swept away on a wave of happiness so massive she wondered if she'd ever come back down to earth.

"I'll take you on, Sheriff," she whispered against his lips. "Forever."

He spun her in a circle as their friends and family cheered. Sienna grinned, realizing she'd found so much more than she'd ever expected in Crimson. A family. A home. And love. Whatever came her way, she could face it fully with Cole by her side. Forever.

* * * * *

Keep reading for a special preview of
HERONS LANDING,
the first in an exciting new series from
New York Times *bestselling author*
JoAnn Ross and HQN Books!

CHAPTER ONE

SETH HARPER WAS spending a Sunday spring afternoon detailing his wife's Rallye Red Honda Civic when he learned that she'd been killed by a suicide bomber in Afghanistan.

Despite the Pacific Northwest's reputation for unrelenting rain, the sun was shining so brightly that the Army notification officers—a man and a woman in dark blue uniforms and black shoes spit-shined to a mirror gloss—had been wearing shades. Or maybe, Seth considered, as they'd approached the driveway in what appeared to be slow motion, they would've worn them anyway. Like armor, providing emotional distance from the poor bastard whose life they were about to blow to smithereens.

At the one survivor grief meeting he'd later attended (only to get his fretting mother off his back), he'd heard stories from other spouses who'd experienced a sudden, painful jolt of loss before their official notice. Seth hadn't received any advance warning. Which was why, at first, the officers' words had been an incomprehensible buzz in his ears. Like distant radio static.

Zoe couldn't be dead. His wife wasn't a combat soldier. She was an Army surgical nurse, working in a heavily protected military base hospital, who'd be returning to civilian life in two weeks. Seth still had a bunch of stuff on his homecoming punch list to do. After buffing the wax off the Civic's hood and shining up the chrome wheels, his next project was to paint the walls white in the nursery he'd added on to their Folk Victorian cottage for the baby they'd be making.

She'd begun talking a lot about baby stuff early in her deployment. Although Seth was as clueless as the average guy about a woman's mind, it didn't take Dr. Phil to realize that she was using the plan to start a family as a touchstone. Something to hang on to during their separation.

In hours of Skype calls between Honeymoon Harbor and Kabul, they'd discussed the pros and cons of the various names on a list that had grown longer each time they'd talked. While the names remained up in the air, she *had* decided that whatever their baby's gender, the nursery should be a bright white to counter the Olympic Peninsula's gray skies.

She'd also sent him links that he'd dutifully followed to Pinterest pages showing bright crib bedding, mobiles and wooden name letters in primary crayon shades of blue, green, yellow and red. Even as Seth had lobbied for Seattle Seahawk navy and action green, he'd known that he'd end up giving his wife whatever she wanted.

The same as he'd been doing since the day he fell head over heels in love with her back in middle school.

Meanwhile, planning to get started on that baby making as soon as she got back to Honeymoon Harbor, he'd built the nursery as a welcome-home surprise.

Then Zoe had arrived at Sea-Tac airport in a flag-draped casket.

And two years after the worst day of his life, the room remained unpainted behind a closed door Seth had never opened since.

MANNION'S PUB & BREWERY was located on the street floor of a faded redbrick building next to Honeymoon Harbor's ferry landing. The former salmon cannery had been one of many buildings constructed after the devastating 1893 fire that had swept along the waterfront, burning down the original wood buildings. One of Seth's ancestors, Jacob Harper, had built the replacement in 1894 for the town's mayor and pub owner, Finn Mannion. Despite the inability of Washington authorities to keep Canadian alcohol from flooding into the state, the pub had been shuttered during Prohibition in the 1930s, effectively putting the Mannions out of the pub business until Quinn Mannion had returned home from Seattle and hired Harper Construction to reclaim the abandoned space.

Although the old Victorian seaport town wouldn't swing into full tourist mode until Memorial Day, nearly every table was filled when Seth dropped in at the end of the day. He'd no sooner slid onto a stool at the end of the long wooden bar when Quinn, who'd been washing glasses in a sink, stuck a bottle of Shipwreck CDA in front of him.

"Double cheddar bacon or stuffed blue cheese?" he asked.

"Double cheddar bacon." As he answered the question, it crossed Seth's mind that his life—what little he had outside his work of restoring the town's Victorian buildings constructed by an earlier generation of Harpers—had possibly slid downhill beyond routine to boringly predictable.

"And don't bother boxing it up. I'll be eating it here," he added.

Quinn lifted a dark brow. "I didn't see that coming."

Meaning that, by having dinner here at the pub six nights a week, the seventh being with Zoe's parents—where they'd recount old memories, and look through scrapbooks of photos that continued to cause an ache deep in his heart—he'd undoubtedly landed in the predictable zone. So, what was wrong with that? Predictability was an underrated concept. By definition, it meant a lack of out-of-the-blue surprises that might destroy life as you knew it. Some people might like change. Seth was not one of them. Which was why he always ordered takeout with his first beer of the night.

The second beer he drank at home with his burger and fries. While other guys in his position might have escaped reality by hitting the bottle, Seth always stuck to a limit of two bottles, beginning with that long, lonely dark night after burying his wife. Because, although he'd never had a problem with alcohol, he harbored a secret fear that if he gave in to the temptation to begin seriously drinking, he might never stop.

The same way if he ever gave in to the anger, the unfairness of what the hell had happened, he'd have to patch a lot more walls in his house than he had those first few months after the notification officers' arrival.

There'd been times when he'd decided that someone in the Army had made a mistake. That Zoe hadn't died at all. Maybe she'd been captured during a melee and no one knew enough to go out searching for her. Or perhaps she was lying in some other hospital bed, her face all bandaged, maybe with amnesia, or even in a coma, and some lab tech had mixed up blood samples with another soldier who'd died. That could happen, right?

But as days slid into weeks, then weeks into months, he'd come to accept that his wife really was gone. Most of the time. Except when he'd see her, from behind, strolling down the street, window-shopping or walking onto the ferry, her dark curls blowing into a frothy tangle. He'd embarrassed himself a couple times by calling out her name. Now he never saw her at all. And worse yet, less and less in his memory. Zoe was fading away. Like that ghost who reputedly haunted Herons Landing, the old Victorian mansion up on the bluff overlooking the harbor.

"I'm having dinner with Mom tonight." And had been dreading it all the damn day. Fortunately, his dad hadn't heard about it yet. But since news traveled at the speed of sound in Honeymoon Harbor, he undoubtedly soon would.

"You sure you don't want to wait to order until she gets here?"

"She's not eating here. It's a command-performance dinner," he said. "To have dinner with her and the guy who may be her new boyfriend. Instead of eating at her new apartment, she decided that it'd be better to meet on neutral ground."

"Meaning somewhere other than a brewpub owned and operated by a Mannion," Quinn said. "Especially given the rumors that said new boyfriend just happens to be my uncle Mike."

"That does make the situation stickier." Seth took a long pull on the Cascadian Dark Ale and wished it was something stronger.

The feud between the Harpers and Mannions dated back to the early 1900s. After having experienced a boom during the end of the nineteenth century, the once-bustling seaport town had fallen on hard times during a national financial depression.

Although the population declined drastically, those

dreamers who'd remained were handed a stroke of luck in 1910 when the newlywed king and queen of Montacroix added the town to their honeymoon tour of America. The couple had learned of this lush green region from the king's friend Theodore Roosevelt, who'd set aside national land for the Mount Olympus Monument.

As a way of honoring the royals, and hoping that the national and European press following them across the country might bring more attention to the town, residents had voted nearly unanimously to change the name to Honeymoon Harbor. Seth's ancestor Nathaniel Harper had been the lone holdout, creating acrimony on both sides that continued to linger among some but not all of the citizens. Quinn's father, after all, was a Mannion, his mother a Harper. But Ben Harper, Seth's father, tended to nurse his grudges. Even century-old ones that had nothing to do with him. Or at least hadn't. Until lately.

"And it gets worse," he said.

"Okay."

One of the things that made Quinn such a good bartender was that he listened a lot more than he talked. Which made Seth wonder how he'd managed to spend all those years as a big-bucks corporate lawyer in Seattle before returning home to open this pub and microbrewery.

"The neutral location she chose is Leaf."

Quinn's quick laugh caused two women who were drinking wine at a table looking out over the water to glance up with interest. Which wasn't surprising. Quinn's brother Wall Street wizard Gabe Mannion might be richer, New York City pro quarterback Burke Mannion flashier, and, last time he'd seen him, which had admittedly been a while, Marine-turned-LA-cop Aiden Mannion had still carried that bad-boy vibe that had gotten him in trouble a lot while they'd been growing up together. But Quinn's superpower had always been the ability to draw the attention of females—from bald babies in strollers to blue-haired elderly women in walkers—without seeming to do a thing.

After turning in the burger order, and helping out his waitress by delivering meals to two of the tables, Quinn returned to the bar and began hanging up the glasses.

"Let me guess," he said. "You ordered the burger as an appetizer before you go off to a vegetarian restaurant to dine on alfalfa sprouts and pretty flowers."

"It's a matter of survival. I spent the entire day until I walked in here taking down a wall, adding a new reinforcing beam and framing out a bathroom. A guy needs sustenance. Not a plate of arugula and pansies."

"Since I run a place that specializes in pub grub, you're not going to get any argument from me on that plan. Do you still want the burger to go for the mutt?"

Bandit, a black Lab/boxer mix so named for his penchant for stealing food from Seth's construction sites back in his stray days—including once gnawing through a canvas ice chest—usually waited patiently in the truck for his burger. Tonight Seth had dropped him off at the house on his way over here, meaning the dog would have to wait a little longer for his dinner. Not that he hadn't mooched enough from the framers already today. If the vet hadn't explained strays' tendencies for overeating because they didn't know where their next meal might be coming from, Seth might have suspected the street-scarred dog he'd rescued of having a tapeworm.

They shot the breeze while Quinn served up drinks, which in this place ran more to the craft beer he brewed in the building next door. A few minutes later, the swinging door to the kitchen opened and out came two layers of prime beef topped with melted local cheddar cheese,

bacon and caramelized grilled onions, with a slice of tomato and an iceberg-lettuce leaf tossed in as an apparent
nod to the food pyramid, all piled between the halves of
an oversize toasted kaiser bun. Taking up the rest of the
heated metal platter was a mountain of spicy French fries.

Next to the platter was a take-out box of plain burger. It
wouldn't stay warm, but having first seen the dog scroung-
ing from a garbage can on the waterfront, Seth figured
Bandit didn't care about the temperature of his dinner.

"So, you're eating in tonight," a bearded giant wearing a T-shirt with Embrace the Lard on the front said in
a deep foghorn voice. "I didn't see that coming."

"Everyone's a damn joker," Seth muttered, even as
the aroma of grilled beef and melted cheese drew him
in. He took a bite and nearly moaned. The Norwegian,
who'd given up cooking on fishing boats when he'd gotten tired of freezing his ass off during winter crabbing
season, might be a sarcastic smart-ass, but the guy sure
as hell could cook.

"He's got a dinner date tonight at Leaf." Quinn, for
some damn reason, chose this moment to decide to get
chatty. "This is an appetizer."

Jarle Bjornstad snorted. "I tried going vegan," he said.
"I'd hooked up with a woman in Anchorage who wouldn't
even wear leather. It didn't work out."

"Mine's not that kind of date." Seth wondered how
much arugula, kale and flowers it would take to fill up
the man with shoulders as wide as a redwood trunk and
arms like huge steel bands. His full-sleeve tattoo boasted
a butcher's chart of a cow. Which might explain his ability to turn a beef patty into something close to nirvana.
"And there probably aren't enough vegetables on the
planet to sustain you."

During the remodeling, Seth had taken out four rows

of bricks in the wall leading to the kitchen to allow the six-foot-seven-inch-tall cook to go back and forth without having to duck his head to keep from hitting the doorjamb every trip.

"On our first date, she cited all this damn research claiming vegans lived nine years longer than meat eaters." Jarle's teeth flashed in a grin in his flaming red beard. "After a week of grazing, I decided that her statistics might be true, but that extra time would be nine horrible baconless years."

That said, he turned and stomped back into the kitchen.

"He's got a point," Quinn said.

"Amen to that." Having learned firsthand how treacherous and unpredictable death could be, with his current family situation on the verge of possibly exploding, Seth decided to worry about his arteries later and took another huge bite of beef-and-cheese heaven.

Need to know what happens next?
Order your copy of HERONS LANDING
wherever you buy your books!

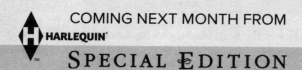

COMING NEXT MONTH FROM

HARLEQUIN®

SPECIAL EDITION

Available June 19, 2018

#2629 A MAVERICK TO (RE)MARRY

Montana Mavericks: The Lonelyhearts Ranch • by Christine Rimmer

Not only were Derek Dalton and Amy Wainwright once an item, they were actually married! With Amy back in town for her friend's wedding, how long before their secret past is revealed?

#2630 DETECTIVE BARELLI'S LEGENDARY TRIPLETS

The Wyoming Multiples • by Melissa Senate

Norah Ingalls went to bed a single mom of triplets—and woke up married! They might try to blame it on the spiked punch, but Detective Reed Barelli is finding it impossible to walk away from this instant family!

#2631 HOW TO ROMANCE A RUNAWAY BRIDE

Wilde Hearts • by Teri Wilson

Days before she turns thirty, Allegra Clark finds herself a runaway bride! Lucky for her, she accidentally crashes a birthday party for Zander Wilde—the man who promised to marry her if neither of them was married by thirty...

#2632 THE SOLDIER'S TWIN SURPRISE

Rocking Chair Rodeo • by Judy Duarte

Erica Campbell is only here to give army pilot Clay Matthews the news: she's having his babies. Two of them! But can she count on Clay—a man whose dreams of military glory have just been dashed—to be her partner in parenthood?

#2633 THE SECRET SON'S HOMECOMING

The Cedar River Cowboys • by Helen Lacey

Jonah Rickard, the illegitimate son of J. D. O'Sullivan, wants nothing to do with his "other" family. Unfortunately, he's falling for Connie Bedford, who's practically part of the family, and he'll have to confront his past to claim the future he wants.

#2634 THE CAPTAIN'S BABY BARGAIN

American Heroes • by Merline Lovelace

After one hot night, Captain Suzanne Hall remembers everything she craved about her sexy ex-husband. Now she's pregnant and Gabe thinks they should get married...again! Will they be able to overcome everything that tore them apart before?

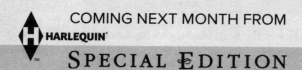

YOU CAN FIND MORE INFORMATION ON UPCOMING HARLEQUIN® TITLES, FREE EXCERPTS AND MORE AT WWW.HARLEQUIN.COM.

HSECNM0618

Is that what you want? The question was still there, in his
eyes. All she had to do was decide.

She took a deep breath and shook her head.

Zander leaned closer, his eyes hard on hers. Then he
reached to cup her face with his free hand and drew the
pad of his thumb slowly, deliberately along the swell of
her bottom lip. "Tell me what you want, Allegra."

You. She swallowed. *I want you.*

"This," she said, reaching up on tiptoe to close the
space between them and touch her lips to his.

What are you doing? Stop.

But it was too late to change her mind. Too late to
pretend she didn't want this. Because the moment her
mouth grazed Zander's, he took ownership of the kiss.

His hands slid into her hair, holding her in place, while
his tongue slid brazenly along the seam of her lips until
they parted, opening for him.

Then there was nothing but heat and want and the
shocking reality that this was what she'd wanted all
along. Zander.

Had she always felt this way? It seemed impossible. Yet beneath the newness of his mouth on hers and the crush of her breasts against the solid wall of his chest, there was something else. A feeling she couldn't quite put her finger on. A sense of belonging. Of destiny.

Home.

Allegra squeezed her eyes closed. She didn't want to imagine herself fitting into this life again. There was too much at stake. Too much to lose. But no matter how hard she railed against it, there it was, shimmering before like her a mirage.

She whimpered into Zander's mouth, and he groaned in return, gently guiding her backward until her spine was pressed against the cool marble wall. Before she could register what was happening, he gathered her wrists and pinned them above her head with a single, capable hand. And the last remaining traces of resistance melted away. She couldn't fight it anymore. Not from this position of delicious surrender. Her arms went lax, and somewhere in the back of her mind, a wall came tumbling down.

The breath rushed from her body, and a memory came into focus with perfect, crystalline clarity.

Let's make a deal. If neither of us is married by the time we turn thirty, we'll marry each other. Agreed?

Agreed?

THE WORLD IS BETTER WITH

Romance

Harlequin has everything from contemporary, passionate and heartwarming to suspenseful and inspirational stories.

Whatever your mood, we have a romance just for you!

Connect with us to find your next great read, special offers and more.

LOVE
Harlequin
romance?

Join our Harlequin community to share your thoughts and connect with other romance readers!

Be the first to find out about promotions, news, and exclusive content!

Sign up for the Harlequin e-newsletter and download a free book from any series at

www.TryHarlequin.com

CONNECT WITH US AT:

Harlequin.com/Community

 Facebook.com/HarlequinBooks

 Twitter.com/HarlequinBooks

 Instagram.com/HarlequinBooks

 Pinterest.com/HarlequinBooks

ReaderService.com

**ROMANCE WHEN
YOU NEED IT**

Earn points from all your Harlequin book purchases from wherever you shop.

Turn your points into *FREE BOOKS* of your choice
OR
EXCLUSIVE GIFTS from your favorite authors or series.

Join for FREE today at
www.HarlequinMyRewards.com.

Harlequin My Rewards is a free program (no fees) without any commitments or obligations.